Pet Finders Club

Help Find Honey!

by Ben M. Baglio

Cover art by Andrew Beckett
Interior art by Doris Ettlinger

SCHOLASTIC INC.

New York   Toronto   London   Auckland   Sydney
Mexico City   New Delhi   Hong Kong   Buenos Aires

Special thanks to Liss Norton

ISBN 0-439-87143-3

Text copyright © 2006 by Working Partners Limited.
Illustrations copyright © 2006 by Scholastic Inc.

All rights reserved. Published by Scholastic Inc.

SCHOLASTIC and associated logos are trademarks and/or
registered trademarks of Scholastic Inc.

12 11 10 9 8 7 6 5 4 3 2 1   6 7 8 9 10 11/0

Printed in the U.S.A.
First Scholastic printing, September 2006

Orchard • Park's • 1st Annual DOG SHOW

Chapter One

"Jet's doing great, isn't he, Buddy?" Andi Talbot said to her cute tan-and-white Jack Russell terrier. She and Buddy were checking out the Basic Obedience class at the ASPCA center in Orchard Park while they waited for their Musical Freestyling lesson to begin.

Andi's good friend, Natalie, and her black Labrador, Jet, had been attending the obedience class for a few months, and Andi could really see the difference in Jet's behavior—right then, for instance. The owners were lining up their dogs along the far side of the hall. Jet was in the middle of the line watching Natalie intently.

"Sit, Jet," said Natalie.

Jet obediently folded his haunches underneath him. Natalie unclipped his leash, gave him the command to "stay," and walked away. The other dogs scampered after their owners, but Jet stayed put.

"That's terrific, Natalie!" Fisher Pearce called from the other end of the hall. He was the tall, good-looking ASPCA veterinarian who ran the obedience classes. "When you think what he used to be like . . . !"

"Hey, don't remind her!" Andi grinned as Natalie rolled her eyes. It was hard to believe that not long ago Natalie couldn't let Jet off his leash because he'd probably have run off and gotten lost. In fact, it was after one of Jet's solo adventures that Andi and Nat had become friends.

Buddy had gotten lost, too, and while Andi and their friend, Tristan, were searching for him, they'd found Jet! Soon after, the three of them formed the Pet Finders Club and together had solved tons of missing animal cases.

Natalie reached the far side of the hall and turned back to Jet. "Here, boy," she called, patting her leg. Jet charged toward her, bounding over a plump Pekinese. He launched himself at Natalie and sent her staggering back against the wall.

"Whoa!" Natalie laughed. When she'd regained her balance, she patted the panting dog's neck. "Good boy, Jet. But could you try being a bit less enthusiastic next time?"

Fisher clapped his hands. "Can I have everyone's attention, please?"

The dog owners clipped their pet's leashes on and turned toward Fisher.

"Christine Wilson from Paws for Thought should be by any moment with entry forms for the first-ever Orchard Park Pet Show. I hope you'll all enter your dogs and any other pets you might—ah, here she is!"

Christine was backing into the hall carrying one end of a heavy box. Tristan held the other end.

Andi felt a thrill of excitement. Christine and Fisher had been working out the details of this show for weeks. It was part of a national program of shows sponsored by the ASPCA. It had even been advertised on TV, to attract people with pedigree pets who were regulars on the show circuit. Now, at last, Andi would find out all about Orchard Park's event. "Come on, Bud," she said, darting across the hall to help.

"Please pick up leaflets and entry forms as you leave. I'll see you all next week," Fisher told the students. "Natalie, can I see you for a moment?"

"Sure." Natalie crossed the room with Jet by her side.

Tristan and Christine lowered the box of Pet Show details onto a table near the door. "Wow," Tristan said, shaking out his hands. "I never realized paper could be so heavy."

People began to gather around the table, and Andi grabbed a bunch of leaflets to hand out.

"There's a Basic Obedience class in the show," Christine said to the dog owners. "A class is a grouping of competitors. Maybe some of you would like to enter that one. There's a class for the prettiest dog, too, as well as the more usual pet-show classes for pedigrees, of course. The ASPCA wants to give people with regular pets the chance to compete alongside serious competitors so that everyone sees how much fun dog shows can be."

Andi gave out the last of her leaflets then grabbed one for herself. There were so many classes; she wasn't sure which was the best one for Buddy to enter.

Tristan read the list over her shoulder. "Nothing for snakes or reptiles," he said, disappointed. "Too bad. That would have been worth seeing."

"They'll all be worth seeing," Andi pointed out.

Natalie came racing over with Jet at her heels. "Guess what? Jet's been recommended for the Intermediate Obedience course!"

"That's awesome!" Tristan cried.

"Good old Jet!" Andi exclaimed, patting him. "Hey,

Nat. You should try this event—the Junior Dog Handler category." She pointed to a line on her leaflet. "And Tris, your cat, Lucy, has to be in the cat class."

"Maybe," Tristan replied. "But she gets a ton of attention already from being in those cat-food commercials. Any more, she might start thinking she's a diva!"

"I think Jet and Buddy should *both* enter the Junior Dog Handling," Fisher said, coming over.

"Me, too," Christine agreed, tucking a lock of thick black hair behind her ear. "The show organizers are especially eager for kids to get involved, which is why they've provided some special classes. You'll have to walk your dogs around the floor at different speeds, get them to change direction, and to heel . . . that sort of thing."

"Buddy could totally do that," Andi said, making up her mind to put his name down.

Natalie shook her head. "I don't know if Jet's ready to perform in front of strangers."

"He'll be fine," Fisher said. "And the judges will be looking at how the handlers work their dogs. They won't expect polished show-ring performances."

"We're going to have each dog do a little trick, too," Christine continued.

Andi had never tried teaching Buddy a trick before,

but she didn't see why he couldn't learn one for the show. In fact, teaching him would be fun. "Buddy would love that."

Natalie frowned. "That sounds hard." She took the leaflet from Andi and scanned it. "Now *this* is perfect for Jet: Best Condition Dog. Doesn't he have the glossiest fur you've ever seen?"

"The judges won't be looking only at a dog's appearance," Fisher said. "They'll want to see how well he interacts with you. And how well he behaves while he's being shown."

"Hey guys," Chloe, the Musical Freestyling teacher entered the hall with Purdy, her cream Pomeranian. "Has Fisher told you about the freestyling demonstration I'm giving at the Pet Show?"

"No," Andi and Natalie said together.

Chloe stopped beside them. She made a tiny gesture with her hand, and Purdy instantly sat at her feet. "I hoped you two would take part," she said.

"Cool!" Andi exclaimed. She and Buddy loved Musical Freestyling, which was like dancing for dogs. "Come on, Nat! You and Jet have to do it, too. It'll be so much fun!"

Buddy barked twice.

"Okay!" Natalie grinned. "I can see Buddy means business."

A well-dressed man with light brown skin and friendly brown eyes entered the hall, a tiny ball of golden fluff trotting in behind him.

"Oh, wow!" Andi cried when she saw them. "What sort of dog is this?" She knelt beside the tiny creature and held out her hand to be sniffed.

"A long-haired Chihuahua," the man said.

Andi ran her hand gently over the tiny dog's soft fur. "Aren't you cute?" she whispered. The dog wasn't much bigger than one of Andi's mom's fluffy slippers. Her thick fur was mostly golden tan, but her nose, chest, and paws were pure white. Her gorgeous dark eyes gazed up at Andi.

"Hi, Fisher," said the Chihuahua's owner. "I came to pick up a Pet Show entry form."

"Great!" Fisher said. "I hoped you'd enter. Kids, this is David Nazrallah. These three are the Pet Finders—Andi, Tristan, and Natalie. If you ever lose a pet, they're the people to see." He stooped down and ran his fingers along the Chihuahua's back. "This little lady is Supreme Champion High Ridge Honeybee."

"Honey for short," David said.

Andi thought the name suited the dog perfectly: Her fur was the exact color of honey.

Natalie slid onto the floor beside Andi. "I've never

seen a dog this small before. How old is she, Mr. Nazrallah?"

"Almost two. And you can call me David."

Natalie stroked one of Honey's ears. "She's even softer than the angora sweater I bought last week."

Jet reached down to sniff the Chihuahua. "Careful, Jet," Natalie warned. She gently pushed him away. "You'll frighten Honey."

"It's okay," David said. "She loves other dogs."

The little dog boldly trotted to Jet, reaching up to sniff him. Jet lowered his head and touched her nose with his. Buddy just stared at Honey as though trying to figure out what sort of animal she could possibly be.

"Jet looks like a giant next to Honey," Tristan said. "And even old Bud seems big. I'll bet you could carry Honey around in your pocket if you wanted to."

"Not quite." David laughed. "Actually she travels in a dog carrier. I asked Christine for something a bit out of the ordinary, and she came up with a fabulous sparkly pink carrier. It's a bit over the top, but Honey deserves it."

"Does Honey win lots of shows?" Andi asked. She was starting to feel a bit anxious about entering Buddy for the Pet Show now that she knew Honey would be taking part. Buddy was the best dog in the world, but he wasn't exactly showy.

"Quite a few," David said.

Chloe glanced at her watch. "I'd better get started. Can I interest you and Honey in Musical Freestyling, David?"

"No, thanks. It's not really our thing," he replied. "Well, great to meet you all! Come on, Honey." He strode away with the Chihuahua trotting daintily behind him.

"I didn't realize top show dogs would be entering the Pet Show," Andi remarked as Chloe headed to the far end of the hall to prepare for the freestyling lesson. "Buddy's just a regular pet. Maybe I shouldn't enter him."

"Of course you should," Christine said firmly. "The judge will love his personality. And anyway, Honey and Buddy won't be in the same class, if that's what you're worried about." She ruffled Buddy's fur. "If you want to make him look extra good, you can always take him to Clip 'n' Curl."

"Clip 'n' Curl?" Andi echoed.

"It's the new pet-grooming parlor just off Main Street. A friend of mine runs it. She used to be a hairdresser but she likes dogs and cats better than people, so now she pampers them instead. Her name is Aggie Patel."

"Hey, Bud? How about a makeover?" Andi asked.

"I'll take Jet," Natalie decided. "He'll look perfect in the show ring if he's been groomed by an expert. And I'm going to have my mom make *me* an appointment at her real salon."

"Uh-oh," Tristan muttered. "Don't get carried away with the grooming, Nat."

"Don't worry. I don't want Jet and me to have matching manicures or anything. The idea of polishing a dog's claws is totally gross. I mean, what's the point? Jet would probably chip his in seconds!" Natalie winked at Andi as Tristan looked totally horrified at the thought of canine manicures.

Chapter Two

"I can't believe summer is over already!" Andi said the next morning as she, Natalie, and Tristan headed to their first day of the new school year.

"Don't remind me," Tristan said. "I've been trying to forget."

"Hey, Andi, are those new cargo pants?" Natalie asked, stopping for a closer look at Andi's pants. "Nice."

"Thanks," Andi said, glad that Natalie had noticed. "I got them on Saturday." They were a pale sandy color with two roomy buttoned pockets halfway down the legs. "Like my sneakers?" She pulled up her pant legs to reveal a pair of bright red, ankle-high sneakers with white toe caps and laces.

Natalie nodded. "How about my outfit?" She twirled, showing off her black capris and beautiful orange sweater with its narrow black stripe down each sleeve.

"Cute!" Andi said.

As they turned into the school yard, Tristan gave an exaggerated yawn. "Clothes are *so* boring!"

"They're more interesting than *skateboards*," Natalie said, digging him in the ribs. The first bell was ringing and people were already filing into school.

"Hey, who's that?" Tristan asked, pointing to a girl standing alone on the far side of the yard. "I don't recognize her. Do you think she's new?"

"Could be," Andi agreed. The girl was tall and slim with black wavy hair in a high ponytail. She was dressed in a flared raspberry skirt, a black top dotted with shiny white stars, and black knee-high boots. A pure white fleece was slung over her arm.

"Let's find out where she shops!," Natalie whispered, pulling Andi toward the girl.

Tristan groaned.

"Hi!" Natalie called. "I like your outfit."

The girl smiled. "Really? Thanks! I had trouble deciding what to wear for my first day."

"You look awesome," Natalie said. "Where did you—?"

The girl didn't let her finish. "I'm Ella Mendez, by the way. Mr. Robinson is my teacher. Can you show me where to go?"

"I'll show you," Tristan offered. "I'm in Mr. Robinson's class."

"Thanks." Ella beamed at him. "Do any of you live near Oriole Way? We moved there a couple weeks ago."

"Do you live in that big house at the end of the street?" Tristan asked. Ella nodded. "Then it was my parents who sold it to you. They run a real estate business."

"Cool!" Ella did a little jump, setting her pony-tail swinging. "My dad just got a new job running the Orchard Park multiplex. We used to live in Denver, Colorado. What are your names?"

Andi introduced herself and her friends. "Don't worry about being the new kid," she added. "I started here a year ago, and I was really worried my first day. Luckily, I met up with Nat and Tris and we became fast friends. We even formed the Pet Finders Club to help people who've lost their pets."

"Yeah, we're—" Natalie began.

"I *love* animals!" Ellie interrupted. "I was an ASPCA volunteer back in Denver. All those cute little puppies and kittens."

"Too bad you weren't in our class last year," Andi said. "We had the cutest little hamster named Cinnamon."

"A hamster?" Ella cut in. "I love their twinkling eyes and tiny paws."

"Well, I guess we should go in," Andi said, noticing that the yard was almost empty.

"Lead on, Tristan." Ella grabbed his arm and yanked him toward the building.

Tristan glanced back at Andi and Natalie and gave them a goofy smile. "She's nice, right?" he mouthed.

Andi nodded her agreement. "Ella *is* nice," she said to Natalie when the others were out of earshot. "What do you think?"

Natalie shrugged. "She's got good taste, but she sure talks a lot!"

Natalie and Andi's new classroom was large and sunny and overlooked the playing field. They found two empty desks near the window and sat down.

"I'm really glad we're in the same class," said Natalie. "I'd feel like I was starting over if I didn't know anyone in homeroom!"

Andi nodded. Luckily, most of their friends from Mr. Dixon's class would be in the same class this year. Like Natalie, she didn't feel like starting over.

"Where's Cinnamon's cage?" Natalie wondered.

"Howard took Cinnamon home for the summer," Andi remembered. "He's bringing him back today."

Tanya McLennan, one of their classmates from last

year, sat down at the next table. "What do you think the teacher will be like?" she asked Andi.

Andi shrugged. "Don't know."

"Well, I hope she's young and pretty," Natalie said. "Not like Mrs. Swanson. Are we lucky *not* to have her, or what?"

"Totally," Andi agreed. She'd heard horror stories from Tristan's older brother, Dean.

Another one of their classmates, Chen, turned in his seat to speak to them. "I heard our teacher isn't from around here."

Tanya nodded. "She can't be from Orchard Park or she'd have come in last June to meet us."

"Maybe she's from Mars," Andi joked. "And *looks* like a teacher but really wears tons of makeup to hide her green scaly skin."

"Good morning, everyone!" Their new teacher strode into the room and shut the door behind her. She was definitely young, with bright blue eyes and pretty black hair that reached almost to her waist.

"I hope she didn't hear what I said," Andi whispered to Nat.

The teacher set a pile of books on her desk and gazed at the class. "I'm Ms. McNicholas." She waited until everyone was settled then added, "I'm sorry to disap-

point you all, but I am not an alien in disguise." Her eyes
rested briefly on Andi.

Andi gulped. She *had* heard!

The door opened and Howard struggled into the room
carrying a bulging plastic bag. "Sorry," he said. "My
backpack broke just as I was leaving and I had to load
all my stuff in this bag instead."

"No excuses in this classroom," Ms. McNicholas said.
"Make sure you're on time tomorrow. Now, hurry up and
find a free desk and sit down."

Howard turned beet-red. "Yes, Ma'am." At that moment, the plastic bag broke and pens, pencils, and an
apple went shooting across the floor. Andi rose to help
him.

"Young lady, do you have permission to get out of
your seat?" Ms. McNicholas called.

Embarrassed, Andi slid back down. She and Natalie
exchanged surprised glances.

"Looks like we'll have to watch our step with her,"
Natalie whispered.

Chapter Three

"Too bad you guys have a tough teacher like Ms. McNicholas," Tristan said as he, Andi, Natalie, and Ella headed for Clip 'n' Curl after school. "Mr. Robinson seems cool so far."

"Yeah," Ella agreed. "He's just like my old teacher back in Denver—always joking and making everything seem really interesting. And he hasn't given us any homework yet."

"Lucky you." Andi sighed. "Ms. McNicholas has already assigned piles for us."

"Come on, no more talking about school," Tristan said. "When we're finished checking out Clip 'n' Curl, we should give Ella a guided tour of Orchard Park. We'll start at Paws for Thought."

"What's that?" Ella asked.

"Only the best pet shop in Seattle," Natalie replied.

"And you'll get to meet Max, the owner's spaniel," Andi added.

"Um . . . great!" Ella said. "You guys should come to my dad's multiplex. It's got a twelve-screen cinema, bowling, and a bunch of fun places to eat."

"Movies, bowling, and food under one roof. Heaven!" Tristan declared.

A few minutes later they were standing outside the grooming parlor, a brightly lit store with pet accessories displayed in the window.

"Wow, look at that!" Natalie exclaimed, pointing to a pink dog collar studded with sparkly heart-shaped gems.

Tristan laughed. "Jet would hate it! Other dogs would tease him."

Andi pressed her nose to the window. Inside she could see a spacious room with dove-gray walls, a wood floor, and shiny chrome light fixtures. The wall opposite the window was covered with mirrors. Three people, two women, and an older man were grooming dogs at high tables. They were all wearing purple coveralls. A raised bath stood in one corner. At the back of the store was a waiting area where a few people sat with their pets.

Andi felt a thrill of excitement at the thought of picking up some tips for grooming Buddy. "Let's go in."

Ella glanced at her watch. "Oh, no! I have to go. I promised I'd watch my baby brother while my mom goes to the supermarket."

"Can't you come in for a few minutes?" Andi asked. "You'll miss all the dogs."

"I don't think so, but I'll see you tomorrow." Ella sped away.

"Bye!" Tristan called as Andi led the way inside.

"I'll be with you in two seconds!" one woman called. The phone was ringing loudly as she lifted a smooth-coated dachshund down from a table and walked it across to the waiting area.

"This place is very chic," Natalie observed. "It kind of reminds me of my salon."

"Well, you'd better make sure you're in the right place the next time you get your hair cut," Tristan joked. "Or else you might end up with a show clip."

"Sorry to keep you waiting," the woman said, walking over to them. She was small and slim and had dark hair worn in a low bun.

"Are you Aggie?" Tristan asked.

"That's right." Aggie's smile grew broader. "Would you

like to book a grooming session?" She opened a large appointment book that lay on a glass shelf in an arch alcove. The phone rang again, but Aggie let the answering machine take the call.

"I think so," Natalie said. "But we hoped to take a look around first. Christine Wilson told us about the salon."

"Then you must be the Pet Finders. Welcome! I've heard all about you." Aggie gestured to the room. "This is the salon and waiting area." She pointed to a purple velvet curtain that covered a doorway. "The store rooms and kennels are out back."

"Kennels?" Tristan echoed, surprised. "You board dogs here?"

"No, but some people drop off their dogs at the beginning of the day, on their way to work, and pick them up on their way home. We need somewhere to keep the dogs when they're not being groomed."

Aggie headed for the waiting area. A stack of pet magazines was piled on a glass table in the corner and a dried-flower arrangement stood on a shelf above. An elderly lady sat in a white leather chair reading a magazine while a cute West Highland white terrier snoozed at her feet. A middle-aged man and his chocolate Lab sat beside her. Next to him, a teenage girl was putting a tartan coat on the dachshund Aggie had just groomed.

Before Andi could decide which dog to pet first, Aggie said, "I'm ready for Cuddles now, Mrs. Granger." She took the Westie's leash. "Come on, fella."

Andi gave up on her idea of getting to know the waiting dogs. She didn't want to miss out on seeing exactly what went on in a grooming parlor. "Mind if we watch?" she asked.

"Not at all." Aggie introduced the group to Joe and Lena, the other two groomers. Joe was an older man with gray hair, wire-framed glasses, and a friendly smile. Lena, an African-American woman with a thick braid of hair, looked more serious.

Joe was brushing a massive Saint Bernard. Loose hair flew up from the dog's coat with every stroke, and he caught it expertly with the brush before it could settle on her fur again. The Saint Bernard was standing perfectly still, her eyes shut.

"Daphne's a regular," Aggie explained. "Luckily, she's happy to get herself into the bath because she's *way* too heavy for anyone to lift."

Andi glanced at the bath and saw that a set of steps led up to the far end of it. She wished they'd come earlier: It would have been great fun to see the huge Saint Bernard jumping into the water.

At the second table, Lena was clipping the toenails

of a young collie with a shiny brown-and-white coat.

"Doesn't that hurt?" Natalie shuddered as the clippers clicked and a shard of claw dropped onto the table.

"She wouldn't be so calm if it did," Lena said. "You have to clip the very end of the claw, so you don't cut the blood vessel inside the nail. Then she doesn't feel a thing." She finished the collie's last nail. "Good girl, Ruby. Now for your bow." Rows of silky ribbons were displayed at the end of each workstation. Lena snipped off a length of blue ribbon and tied it loosely around Ruby's neck so that it hid the dog's collar. Then she snapped on the collie's leash and lifted her down from the table.

The collie stood in front of a mirror gazing at her reflection. Her tail wagged from side to side. Andi wondered if Ruby knew how beautiful she looked or if she was simply happy because she'd had a great time at the salon. She crouched down to smooth the collie's velvety fur. Ruby turned her head and licked Andi's cheek. Then she looked back at the mirror again.

"Okay, that's enough of you admiring yourself," Lena said.

"Bye, Ruby!" Andi said as Lena led the collie out to the kennels.

"Bath time for you, Cuddles," Aggie said, tying on a

plastic apron. She unhooked the Westie's collar and leash and lifted him into the bath, which held about eight inches of warm, foamy water.

Cuddles sat down looking very contented. "He loves his bath," Aggie said. "Too bad they're not all as easy-going as Cuddles. Sometimes we end up wetter than the dogs!"

"Can we help you?" said Tristan.

"Sure. There are spare aprons in the cupboard next to the tub."

The kids put them on and gathered around the bath.

"First off, we have to rub right through his fur, all the way down to his skin to loosen the dirt. You'd be amazed at how dirty dogs get, even stay-at-homes like Cuddles."

The Pet Finders massaged the little dog gently. His tail wagged under the foamy water.

"Great job!" Aggie said after a few minutes. She pressed a button on the shower attachment and a spray of warm water squirted out.

"Can I rinse him?" Andi asked eagerly. This was the part of his bath Buddy liked best—he made a great game of trying to bite the shower spray.

"Yep." Aggie pulled the plug and the water began to drain. Andi held the shower above Cuddles and let it

rinse away the soapsuds. He sat very still with his eyes closed. "All done, boy," Andi declared when every last bubble had been washed off.

"Thanks," Aggie said as Andi switched off the shower. "Now, out you come, Cuddles." She wrapped a fluffy white towel around him, lifted him out of the tub, and carried him to a grooming station. The Pet Finders helped rub him dry. Cuddles looked at each of them and gave a happy little yap.

When his fur was dry and sticking out all over the place, Aggie dropped the damp towels into a chrome laundry bin under her table. Then she selected a wide-toothed comb from her rack of grooming tools. "First I'll comb him all over," she said, letting the Westie sniff the comb before she started.

They watched carefully as Aggie teased out the tangles. Andi combed and brushed Buddy regularly, but she wanted to learn any new techniques that could help him look his best for the Pet Show.

Lena brought in the chocolate Lab from the waiting area, but Andi hardly noticed. She was too busy watching what Aggie was doing.

Once Cuddles was tangle free, Aggie chose a rubber brush. "Different dogs need different brushes," she explained. "Cuddles has short hair and sensitive skin, so I only use a rubber brush on him." She began to work from the little Westie's head toward his tail and legs. "It's important to go right down to the skin when you brush an animal," she said. "It stimulates the skin and allows natural oils to circulate into its coat. That way, its fur stays healthy and shiny." She paused a moment and parted the hair on Cuddles's left shoulder. "He had a patch of dry skin here last time he came, but it seems to be gone now."

Cuddles's tail wagged nonstop while he was being groomed. He was obviously having a great time.

"There," Aggie said, setting the brush down on the table. "He doesn't need his nails clipped," she added "I just did them a couple of weeks ago. It's just ears now."

Taking a cotton ball from a jar on a shelf underneath the table, she moistened it with olive oil. Then she cleaned gently inside Cuddles's ear. "Do you do that every time?" Andi asked. She'd never used oil on Buddy's ears before.

Aggie nodded. "Oil is a great cleanser."

Andi made up her mind to try it out on Buddy. She was sure he'd enjoy the extra attention. She turned to look at the ribbons, wondering which color Aggie would pick for the finishing touch. *Red would be nice with Cuddles's white fur*, she thought. She noticed an array of pet costumes hanging on a rail behind the ribbon stand. "Look at these," she said, going closer.

Natalie and Tristan followed her.

"Oh, wow!" Natalie held up a doggy sailor suit and hat. "Buddy would love this!"

Tristan snorted. "Yeah, right. He'd jump right into a mud puddle to escape the humiliation."

Andi laughed. Tristan was probably right. There was nothing Buddy liked more than rolling in mud, but, all the same, he'd look adorable with the little sailor hat perched on his head.

"Check this out," Natalie said, holding up a pink ballerina outfit. "And this." She showed them a silver fairy outfit with shimmering wings.

"Don't even think about it," Andi said. "Jet would hate wearing those."

"I guess they *are* a bit over the top," Natalie agreed.

"Over the top and down the other side!" Tristan exclaimed.

"Cuddles is finished now," Aggie called. "Can one of you take him to the waiting area for me while I sterilize my tools?" He was still sitting on the table, but now he was wearing his collar and leash and a red ribbon tied in a neat bow.

"I will," Tristan said, "before these two start dressing him up."

Aggie smiled. "Actually, our pet ensembles are pretty popular. Quite a few of our clients hold doggy costume parties."

Tristan rolled his eyes. "You've got to be kidding me!" he said, and led Cuddles back to his owner.

"Maybe we can help you out, Aggie," Natalie suggested. "You said you were really busy. We could wash the dogs for you and get them from the waiting area and the kennels, while you concentrate on the grooming."

Andi couldn't think of a better way to spend her afternoons. Right now they didn't have any missing pet cases to investigate, but working at Clip 'n' Curl would be the next best thing. They'd get to meet tons of new dogs and maybe a few cats, too.

"That would be fantastic!" Aggie said. "And in return, I'll groom your pets for the Pet Show!"

Andi couldn't believe their luck. They'd have a great time helping out, and Bud, Jet, and Lucy would get free beauty treatments!

Chapter Four

"Come on, Buddy. Just do it once, okay?" Andi begged. It was Friday morning before school and she had been standing in her living room holding a sparkly purple hoop for over an hour. She was trying to teach her dog to jump through it for his special pet show trick. So far, it wasn't working.

"Woof!" Buddy wagged his stumpy tail.

"Go on," Andi said, pushing her hand through the hoop to show him what to do. "Good boy. You can do it."

The little Jack Russell darted forward then ducked underneath the hoop with an excited bark.

Andi lowered the hoop a little. "You have to go *through* it, not underneath."

But Buddy didn't go underneath this time, he dodged around the side!

Andi groaned and rested the hoop on the floor. She

took a dog treat out of her pocket and threw it through the hoop. "Come on, you can do it, Bud."

Buddy trotted up to the hoop and stepped through. He gobbled up the dog treat.

"All right!" Andi cheered. She patted the little terrier and he circled around her legs.

"Now, a little higher." Andi held the hoop an inch off the ground. "Go on, Bud." She tossed a dog treat through again.

Buddy scampered up to the hoop. He stopped and looked up at Andi. "Go on," Andi encouraged him.

Buddy sniffed the hoop then walked around it to get his treat.

"Oh, Bud!" Andi dropped the hoop.

Before Buddy could try again, the doorbell rang. "Here's Nat and Tristan," Andi said, ruffling Buddy's ears. "We'll practice again after dinner if I don't have too much homework. I'm not sure the judges will be impressed with a dog who *walks* through hoops, even if he is the best dog in the world."

"Thank goodness Ella's not in our class," Natalie said, flopping into her desk chair a little while later. Ms. McNicholas was busy opening some of the classroom's windows, so Nat continued to complain a bit.

When Andi had opened her front door that morning, she'd found a smiling Tristan and Ella and a frowning Natalie standing on the porch. They'd come to walk to school with her.

"Why did Tristan have to invite her to walk with us, anyway?" Nat continued. "Who cares if he likes her? I mean, the girl won't let anyone else get a word in. I'll bet she's still talking Tristan's ear off right now!"

Ella did talk a lot, but Andi had a feeling that Natalie was more annoyed at all the attention the new girl was getting.

Before Andi could reply, Ms. McNicholas began to take attendance.

"Okay!" Ms. McNicholas clapped her hands after the last name had been called. "Let's take out our history books. Today we're going to learn about the American colonies."

Andi grabbed her history text, a notebook, and a pen from her desk.

"As you know, Christopher Columbus discovered America in 1492," the teacher began.

"Whoa!" Chen cried out. "He is so cool!"

"Well . . . this is true," Ms. McNicholas said. "Columbus was a very adventurous man."

"No, not him, Ms. McNicholas." Chen shook his head. *"Him!"* He pointed out the window.

Andi instantly spotted what Chen had seen—a beautiful gray parrot with bright red tail feathers swooping across the playground. "Wow!" she gasped.

The bird made a sharp turn and headed straight for the building. It flew closer . . . and closer . . .

Suddenly, Andy heard a fluttering noise at the open window—and the bird flew right into the classroom! *"Aak . . . aak, aak!"*

"Help!" Tanya yelled. Then the whole class jumped up from their seats, shouting and laughing at once.

"Where did it come from?" someone cried.

"Catch it!" another yelled.

The parrot fluttered around the room, squawking loudly. Andi watched it excitedly, hoping it would perch on her desk. But the bird didn't settle anywhere. It soared right up to the ceiling, then skimmed so low they had to duck.

"There it goes!" Chen shouted.

"Silence!" Ms. McNicholas ordered.

In less than ten seconds, the whole class was back in their seats.

In a flash of gray and scarlet, the parrot soared upward, almost brushing the ceiling with its wings before settling on the flagpole at the front of the room.

"Don't make a sound," Ms. McNicholas warned the

class. She stretched out her arm toward the bird. "Come on!" she murmured. "Don't be scared."

Everyone held their breath. Andi wished they could close the windows so the parrot couldn't fly out again, but any movement might frighten it away before they'd had time to close them all.

"Come on," Ms. McNicholas urged. "We won't hurt you."

The parrot blinked a few times then spread its wings and fluttered down to her, its scarlet tail bobbing. It landed on her shoulder.

Ms. McNicholas stroked the parrot's feathery chest. "There, now."

"I guess she knows about birds," Andi whispered to Nat.

"Hammer . . . slammer . . . *aak*," the parrot squawked.

The whole class laughed, including Ms. McNicholas.

"Where did it come from?" Chen asked.

"And what are we going to do with it?" Tanya called. "Can we keep it?"

"What sort of bird is it?" asked someone behind Andi.

"Wait," Ms. McNicholas said, holding up a hand. "I can't answer if you all talk at once."

Everyone stopped talking and waited.

"This is an African gray," Ms. McNicholas said. "And

I don't know where it came from, but we can't keep it, that's for sure. Tanya, will you go to the principal's office and ask her to call the ASPCA?"

Tanya sped out of the room.

"If you're sitting near an open window, shut it now so this little beauty can't fly away before help arrives," Ms. McNicholas continued.

The windows were slammed shut, making the parrot flap its wings in alarm. "It's okay," Ms. McNicholas murmured to the bird.

The parrot settled down again as the teacher smoothed its feathers.

"What are we going to do with it until the ASPCA comes?" said Howard.

"He can sit on my desk." Ms. McNicholas emptied her heavy ceramic pencil cup to use as a perch.

The parrot looked at the pot, tilted its head to one side, then hopped onto it, curling his claws over the rim.

"Perfect," Ms. McNicholas said. "He'll be quite happy there while we get back to the colonies."

"*Aak!*" the parrot squawked as the class got back to their studies.

Andi found it impossible to concentrate on the history lesson. The bird had to be lost—it wouldn't be flying around on its own otherwise. Andi felt a rush of excitement at the thought of another investigation for the PFC.

She studied the parrot as it perched on the edge of the cup. Its feathers were in good condition, glossy and smooth, and its eyes were bright. It was clearly well cared for. *It doesn't look thin or hungry*, Andi thought, *so it can't have been missing for long.*

"Adam and Eve on a raft! Hammer slammer! *Aak!*" the parrot squawked. A wave of giggles erupted around the room.

"What on Earth?" Natalie whispered.

Andi shrugged. She glanced at the clock, impatient for morning recess to start. She couldn't wait to tell Tristan that the Pet Finders were on a new case!

Unfortunately, Ms. McNicholas had the class work through morning recess to make up for the time they'd lost over the parrot. When lunchtime came, Andi and Natalie raced out to the yard to find Tristan. He was talking to a group of friends.

"Tris, the Pet Finders have a new case!" Natalie announced.

"An African gray parrot flew into our classroom this morning," Andi explained.

"Whoa! That's amazing!" Ella's voice sounded.

Natalie's smile faded as the new girl appeared from behind Tristan.

"Tell us everything," Ella demanded. "Where did it come from?"

"We don't know yet," Andi replied.

"We could try the zoo," Tristan suggested.

Natalie rummaged through her backpack and pulled out her cell phone. "I'll look up the number on the Internet and give them a call."

"Don't bother. The zoo doesn't have any African grays," Ella said. "My dad took us last weekend."

Natalie frowned, but Tristan said, "Thanks, Ella. That saved us a phone call."

Andi spotted Fisher coming out of the school then, carrying a travel cage. To her surprise, the cage was empty. "There's Fisher," she said. "But where's the parrot?"

The Pet Finders and Ella pelted across the schoolyard.

"Hey, guys," said Fisher.

"Aren't you taking the parrot away?" Natalie asked.

"No. Nobody's reported a parrot missing, so Ms. McNicholas offered to look after him for now. She used to keep exotic birds, so she knows what she's doing. I'll bring a cage over for him later."

"She won't need to look after him for long," Ella said. "Now that *we're* on the case!"

"Oh?" Natalie wondered. "Who said you were in the Pet Finders Club?"

"Uh, we can always use some extra help," Tristan stuttered. "Let's go take a look at the parrot. Maybe we'll find a clue about where it came from."

"Oh, wait. I forgot. I have to go to the library," Ella said, looking at her feet. "I have to do some reading, but I'll see you guys later, okay? I'll want to hear everything!"

"So now you don't want to be a Pet Finder?" Natalie queried, raising her eyebrows.

"Totally, but this assignment can't wait. See you!" Ella ran off.

The Pet Finders crept back into Andi and Natalie's classroom and found the parrot walking back and forth along the edge of Ms. McNicholas's desk. A few sunflower seeds were scattered on the tabletop and he stopped to eat one. "*Aak!* Adam and Eve on a raft! *Aak!*" he cried.

"Adam and Eve on a raft?" Tristan echoed. "What does that mean?"

"No idea," Natalie said with a shrug.

"Maybe he came to Orchard Park on a boat," Andi suggested.

"Why a boat when he can fly?" Tristan said.

"I wonder who Adam and Eve are?" Natalie said, shutting the door carefully so the parrot couldn't escape. "Two other birds, maybe?"

"Weird names for owners," Andi said as the kids tiptoed toward the teacher's desk.

The parrot spread his wings and took off. He completed a circuit of the room, then swooped low over Tristan's head and landed on the desk again. "Italian scallion. *Aak!*"

"Italian stallion?" Tristan said. "Maybe his owner has a horse, too."

"It said *scallion*." Natalie giggled. "Not stallion."

Stroking the bird's soft feathery head with one finger, Andi studied him to see if he had any special markings or an ID tag. She noticed a small gold-colored ring around its leg with a tiny gold palm tree attached.

"That's got to be a clue," Natalie said.

"It'll be a good security check, too," Tristan said. "If anyone calls to claim the parrot, we can ask what it wears on its leg. Parrots are pretty valuable; we don't want to give it to the wrong person."

"Good thinking," Andi told him.

"I'll take a picture for some lost parrot posters," Natalie said, flipping her cell phone open. As she snapped the photo, Ms. McNicholas came in.

"What are you kids doing in here?" she asked, surprised.

"We're the Pet Finders Club," Andi explained, "and we're looking for clues so we can track down the parrot's owner."

Ms. McNicholas frowned. "What are you talking about?"

Tristan whipped a flyer out of his backpack and held it out to her. A black-and-white photo showed Andi, Tristan, and Natalie standing in a row with their arms crossed and their faces determined. LOST A PET? WHO YOU GONNA CALL? was printed across the top. At the bottom, in big, bold letters, was written PET FINDERS!

"Hmm. I see," said Ms. McNicholas. Her mouth twitched as if she was trying not to smile. "Very professional. I'm sure you'll be able to find Charlie's owner—but don't let the search interfere with your schoolwork."

"Charlie?" Natalie said.

"I had a green-wing macaw named Charlie when I was a little girl. I thought I'd call this one the same until we find out his real name."

"You seem to know a lot about parrots," Andi said.

"Can you tell us about their behavior? Do they fly away from home a lot? And if they do, do they try to find their way home again?"

"Grays are very cautious birds, and they're loyal to their owners. It's very rare for one to fly away."

"Well, this one did," Tristan pointed out. "And it's up to us to make sure he gets home again."

Chapter Five

The Pet Finders were still talking about the lost parrot as they headed for Clip 'n' Curl the next morning. "Charlie's owner must really miss him," Andi said.

They arrived at the grooming parlor a few minutes before nine, just as Aggie was letting in the first customers of the day. She stopped to fuss over Jet and Buddy. "Hi, guys! Aren't you adorable?" Buddy and Jet wagged their tails in agreement.

Inside the salon, Joe and Lena were already at their stations, laying out brushes for their first clients.

Joe waved. "Have you brought in Buddy and Jet to be groomed?"

Buddy jerked back on his leash and Andi laughed. "It's okay, boy!" she said. "Not today."

Jet hid behind Tristan and Natalie, trying—and failing—to look small.

"I thought Buddy liked being bathed," Natalie said as Tristan helped her pull Jet inside.

Andi picked up Buddy and carried him through the door. "He does, usually. I guess he doesn't like the look of all those brushes."

"Or maybe he saw the costumes!" Tristan joked.

"Why don't you put the two of them out back in the kennels?" Aggie suggested.

Once they were outside the salon, the dogs relaxed. They trotted into the kennel area, a wide sunny room with patio doors that looked out over the backyard. A stack of glittery, deluxe pet carriers in an assortment of colors was against the far wall. There were four pens in the kennels, all of them large enough to hold two dogs, and each contained a comfortable doggy quilt, a water bowl, and a few toys.

They placed the dogs in the sunniest pen, next to the window. Jet settled down on the cozy quilt, perfectly happy, and Buddy snuggled up beside him.

"Let's go dog washing!" Andi said.

The Pet Finders headed back to the salon and put on plastic aprons.

A moment later the door opened and David Nazrallah walked in carrying a glittery pink dog carrier and a matching case. "Hello," he said. "I didn't know you helped out here."

"We just started," Tristan told him.

David opened the case. "I've brought everything she'll need. Herbal shampoo, some of her favorite snacks, and her towel." He laid them on Aggie's workstation.

Andi ran a warm bath, adding a generous squirt of Honey's shampoo. When the water was ready, she lifted Honey in and began to wash her, working the lather right down to her skin as Aggie had shown her.

"I guess you won't need any help here," Natalie said. "Honey's so small you could wash her one-handed. I'll go see who's next for grooming."

Lena led a bearded collie over from the waiting area. "Tristan, could you help me hold Digby, please? He's only come in for an eyebrow trim, but he can never sit still when I have clippers in my hand."

Tristan helped her lift the shaggy dog onto her work-table.

"We'll have to get going on the parrot posters soon, Andi," Tristan reminded her over Digby's head.

"All done," Andi said. "Nat e-mailed me the picture last night, and I printed the posters this morning."

"Cool!" said Tristan.

"I can't stop thinking about that palm-tree charm," Andi went on. "I'm sure you're right about it being a clue. But what does it mean? Maybe Charlie's owner comes from someplace tropical."

"Or maybe his owner is crazy about coconuts," Tristan offered.

When Honey was clean, Andi pulled out the bath plug and switched on the shower. With a high-pitched yap, Honey scampered into the spray of warm water. She spun around in a circle, shaking droplets all over Andi.

Laughing, Andi rinsed off the last of the lather, switched off the shower, and grabbed Honey's fluffy towel. The little Chihuahua seized the corner of the towel in her teeth and yanked it playfully. *Honey might be a champion show dog, but she knows how to play just like any regular pet*, Andi thought, pleased.

She wrapped Honey in the towel and carried her across to Aggie's grooming table. She rubbed Honey gently, then unwrapped her. The little dog's damp hair stood out in golden, hedgehog spikes.

Natalie came back from the waiting area with a cute tan-and-white cocker spaniel. "He's got some burrs tangled in his coat, Joe. His owner hoped you could get them out without giving him a haircut," she said, handing him the leash. "Oh, doesn't Honey look sweet," she went on, catching sight of the Chihuahua. "Can we style her hair for you, Aggie?"

"After I've clipped her," Aggie said. "If that's all right with you, David."

"That's fine," David replied. "I'm sure you'll make her look great."

"Does she want to wear one of the costumes?" Natalie asked hopefully.

"No, thanks." David laughed. "I think she'll be happier with a nice pink bow to match her carrier and towel."

Tristan came over. The bearded collie's eyebrows had been trimmed and he was sitting happily while Lena brushed his long fur.

"How's Ella, Tris?" Andi asked, grabbing a broom to sweep up fallen hair from the floor.

Tristan looked puzzled. "Okay, I guess. Or at least she was yesterday, at school."

"When's your date?" Natalie said sarcastically, stopping on her way across the salon carrying an armful of clean towels.

Tristan blushed. "What?"

"I think you have a crush on her, Tris," Andi teased.

Tristan's face reddened. "No way!"

"You're right, Andi," Natalie agreed. "Anyone can see it." She gave Andi an exaggerated wink.

Tristan snatched the broom from Andi and began sweeping under Joe's workstation. "We should be talking about the parrot," he said. "Let's go to the Banana Beach Café when we're finished here. Maggie and Jango might be able to give us some hints on finding Charlie's owner."

"Good idea," Andi said.

"I called the zoo," Natalie said, "even though Ella said not to bother."

"Well?" Andi asked.

"Ella was right. They don't have any African grays."

"And Charlie isn't from Paws for Thought or Christine would have told us," Andi said, thinking out loud. "So, he must be someone's pet."

"Someone who likes palm trees," Tristan said. He swept a pile of hair into a dustpan and deposited it in the bin.

"Honey's ready, girls," Aggie called. She'd brushed the Chihuahua's fur until it was smooth and shiny. "She's still a little damp in places," she added, "so you could finish her off with the hair dryer."

Natalie fetched the brush Aggie had been using on Honey—a soft bristle one—and Andi plugged in the hairdryer.

Honey stood patiently while they brushed her hair this way and that, trying to decide which style suited her best. Just as Andi directed the hair dryer onto Honey's chest, a tall woman carrying a white pet carrier burst through the salon door. A tiny black-and-white dog peeped out through the carrier's grille.

"Hello, Amanda," Aggie greeted the woman. "I'm not quite ready for you. Would you mind taking Windwhistle into the waiting area?"

"Actually, I would. You know he hates waiting, and *we're* on time." The woman let her gaze fall on Andi and Natalie. "New staff, I see," she said. "I'm Mrs. Singer and this—" she opened the pet carrier and lifted out her dog, another longhaired Chihuahua "—this is Windwhistle. Take a good look, because he'll soon be the champion of the Orchard Park Pet Show!"

"Now, Amanda," David said, sliding off the chrome stool where he'd been watching Honey have her grooming session. "There are plenty of other dogs in Windwhistle's class. Anyone could win it—including Honey." He was smiling, but Andi could see that he was annoyed by Amanda Singer's boast.

"Don't be so sure, David. Lydia Baxter is judging the miniature dogs," said Mrs. Singer. "And she has spoken very highly of Windwhistle." She held the Chihuahua close to her face. "Isn't that right, precious? My little poppet's going to win first prize, isn't he?"

Windwhistle's tiny tail began to wag.

"There, he knows who's champ," Mrs. Singer cooed.

"We'll see," David said.

Andi and Natalie finished styling Honey's fur and stood back to admire her. Her gold-and-white fur was smooth on her body but they'd fluffed it out around her head like a lion's mane. Natalie had sprayed on a little non-scented hairspray to keep it in place. Andi cut off a length of pink ribbon and tied it around Honey's neck before presenting her to David.

"She looks beautiful," he declared. "You've done a wonderful job, girls."

"Thanks!" said Natalie. "Honey is so sweet, I'm sure she'll be good competition for Windwhistle," she added loyally.

That got Andi thinking. What if all the dogs at the Orchard Park Pet Show were this well-bred and pampered? Would scruffy, lovable Buddy stand a chance of winning a prize at all?

"I love helping out at the grooming parlor," Andi announced as the Pet Finders headed for the Banana Beach Café for lunch.

"Aggie seems pretty happy about it, too," Natalie said.

They reached the café, and Andi and Tristan went

inside, leaving Natalie outside with Buddy and Jet.

"Hey, where have you been?" Maggie Pearce greeted them, wiping her hands on her bright floral apron. "Jango and I haven't seen you for a while."

"We're back at school now," Tristan said, "but we're working on a new pet-finding case — or actually, an *owner*-finding case."

"We found a parrot," Andi added. "We thought you might be able to help us."

Long John Silver, Maggie and Jango's beautiful blue-and-green parrot, fluttered down onto the counter. "More bananas!" he squawked.

"We'll be glad to help if we can," Maggie said. "Do you want anything to eat or drink? We're making great chicken wraps today."

"Yes, please," Andi said. "And we'll all have banana spice smoothies."

"Sit yourselves down," Maggie said, "and I'll bring them out to you. Then Jango and I will have time to chat."

Andi and Tristan joined Natalie outside at a table shaded by a rainbow-striped umbrella. Buddy jumped up, planting his paws on Andi's knee.

Andi patted him then dove into her backpack and

pulled out a stack of pink papers. "Here. I made these last night."

HAVE YOU LOST A PARROT? was written at the top in bold letters. Below was the color photo Natalie had taken with her cell phone, showing Charlie on Ms. McNicholas's desk. The picture was a little fuzzy but still showed the parrot's gray plumage and scarlet tail. Andi's phone number was printed at the bottom of the poster.

Jango Pearce, Maggie's husband, came out of the café carrying three plates. A yellow apron stretched tightly across his belly and his graying hair stood on end, as if he had been running his hands through it. "Did I hear you're looking for a lost parrot?" he asked, setting their plates down on the table.

"No, we've found a parrot and need to track down the owner," Natalie corrected him. "You haven't heard of anyone who's lost an African gray, have you, Jango?"

He shook his head. "Sorry. But I'll put some posters up for you."

"This bird is a real talker," Andi said. Another thought struck her. "Hey, maybe it could tell us its address."

Jango laughed. "Parrots don't really talk. They just copy what they hear. Take Long John Silver, for instance: He says 'more bananas' because he hears Maggie say that all day."

Maggie brought out the smoothies. "My aunt had a parrot," she said, sitting in the empty chair at their table. "It used to make barking noises because her neighbor's dog barked nonstop."

"And my musician friend's parrot, he sounds just like a guitar," Jango added.

Natalie groaned. "So all that stuff Charlie says doesn't mean anything? It's useless."

"No, it's not!" Andi exclaimed, almost choking on her chicken wrap. "It could be a really important clue!" She pulled a scrap of paper out of her pocket. "Quick, let's write down everything he's said!"

Maggie handed her a pen.

"He says, 'Adam and Eve on a raft' a lot," Natalie said.

Andi scribbled it down.

"And 'hammer slammer' and 'Italian scallion,'" Tristan added. "But how could that be important? It's just gibberish."

"Don't you see?" Andi said. "All we have to figure out is where he learned that stuff and the case will be solved!"

Chapter Six

The next morning, the Pet Finders met at nine-thirty to hang up posters about the parrot.

"Let's put one in Rocky's store," Tristan suggested. A friendly woman named Rocky Brand ran a convenience store not far from Andi's house, and she was always willing to display a Pet Finders poster.

As they reached the store, Ms. McNicholas came out carrying a newspaper. "Well, hello," she said. "You guys look like you're on a mission. Any luck finding Charlie's owner?"

"Not yet," Andi replied. "But we made some posters." She handed one to the teacher.

"This looks terrific," Ms. McNicholas said. "My guess is that it won't be long before I lose my new feathered friend." She smiled, but Andi wondered if their teacher was hoping they wouldn't find the parrot's owner too soon. "I brought him home for the weekend," Ms. McNicholas went on. "Would you like to visit him?"

"You bet!" the Pet Finders cried.

"Let me just take this poster inside," Tristan said. He darted into the store and a moment later was out again, posterless. "Rocky's going to hang it for us."

"Great!" Andi said.

It took only a few minutes to walk to Ms. McNicholas's condo, which was on a small block not far from Andi's house. "Up here," the teacher said, leading the way to the second floor and unlocking a blue front door.

Half-filled boxes were everywhere and the living room table was covered in rolls of pale green wallpaper and cans of paint. Beside them, a small box of nails and a hammer were spilling out of a bag from the local home-improvement store. "As you can see, I'm still settling in," Ms. McNicholas said.

Charlie sat on the perch in a large cage by the window, looking very much at home.

"I'll let him out," Ms. McNicholas said. "He could stand to stretch his wings." She opened the cage door.

Charlie hopped down to the doorway and peeked outside the cage before spreading his wings and flying across the room. "Adam and Eve on a raft!" he squawked as he landed on the table beside some rolls of sage-green wallpaper.

"Cool wallpaper," Tristan said.

"Thanks," Ms. McNicholas said. "I'm putting it in here with matching green paint on the door and window frames."

"Paint it red!" Charlie squawked, flying to the curtain pole. "Short lumberjack!"

Andi laughed. "That bird is crazy!"

"Maybe he's trying to make a point about my home decor," Ms. McNicholas joked. "Perhaps he's not keen on green."

"Maybe he belongs to a decorator or a lumberjack?" Tristan suggested.

"Hammer slammer!" shrieked Charlie. "Hammer slammer!"

Natalie gave a squeal. "Of course! Interior decorators use paint, lumberjacks work with timber, and carpenters use hammers."

"Whoa!" Andi exclaimed, patting Natalie on the back. "You might have something there!"

"But where do Adam and Eve fit in?" Tristan asked.

"Maybe Charlie heard that from someone else," Natalie said. "Anyway, it might be worth going to the hardware store and asking if any of the staff lost a parrot."

"DIY Depot is the one closest to the school," Tristan said. "We should start there."

"We can go right away," Ms. McNicholas said. "I need wallpaper supplies anyway." She stretched her arm out to Charlie and the parrot flew down, landing on her wrist. "Let's put you back in your cage, boy," she said, petting his feathery head.

"Paint it red! Paint it red!" Charlie squawked as Ms. McNicholas carried him to the cage.

The teacher laughed. "Sorry, Charlie, no can do. This room's going to be green, and that's that!"

Ms. McNicholas's car was parked in the lot behind the condos. "Wow!" Tristan whispered, impressed. It was a shiny red Corvette with cream leather seats.

"What a great car!" Tristan whistled.

Ms. McNicholas smiled. "Thanks. My father spent ten years restoring it and gave it to me when I gradu-ated. I have to say, it's one of the things I love most in the world!" She opened the passenger door. "The only downside is that it's a long way from being a minivan! I'm afraid two of you will have to squash in the back."

"I'm in front!" Tristan said quickly.

Andi and Natalie clambered into the back of the car. There was hardly any room for them, and they had to sit with their knees almost up to their chins. Not that Andi minded being a bit uncomfortable—not when they might be about to crack a case.

"This car is so cool," Tristan said, settling himself in the front seat. He ran his fingers over the cream dashboard. "I want one exactly like it when I'm old enough to drive."

"I won't be getting any rides from you, then," Natalie said. "Not if I have to sit in the back."

"I might not offer you one," Tristan replied.

It took about five minutes to reach the DIY Depot, a large warehouse set in a huge parking lot. Ms. McNicholas parked beside a pickup truck and they all scrambled out.

Inside, the store was packed, but to Andi's delight she spotted a rack of promising books beside the door. "Check it out," she said, scanning the titles. *"How to Build a Cage for Your Bird*, *Decorating for Bird Lovers*, *Tropical Décor* . . . looks like a bird lover chose to sell these books!"

They hurried to the customer service desk to ask if anyone on the staff owned a parrot while Ms. McNicholas went off to find her tools.

"A parrot? I can't stand birds," the saleswoman said with a shudder. "All that fluttering!"

"But do you know anyone on the staff who owns one?" Andi prompted her.

The woman frowned. "No one that I know of."

"What about all the decorating books for bird lovers?" Tristan asked, pointing to the rack.

"Some of our customers buy them," the woman said with a shrug. "That's why we sell them."

"Looks like a dead end." Natalie sighed as they left the desk, but the cashier called them back.

"Hang on! I think Harry might have some birds. He works in the lumber section at the back of the store."

"Lumber!" Tristan whispered. "Our bird loves that word!"

They raced to the back of the store and found an older man in brown overalls restocking some lumber.

They stepped forward.

"Excuse me, are you Harry?" Natalie asked.

The man turned and ran a hand through his wispy gray hair. "Sure am. Can I help you?"

"The cashier said you might have some birds. We found a lost parrot." Tristan pulled a poster out of his backpack. "We thought it might be yours."

Harry waved the poster away. "Sorry, son. I have a few canaries, but no parrots."

Andi's heart sank. The trail had gone cold again.

Ms. McNicholas was waiting for them at the front of the store. "No luck?" she guessed when she spotted their gloomy faces. "I suppose it was a bit of a long shot."

But as they exited the store, a breeze sprung up and blew across the parking lot. Andi watched an empty soda can rattle across the blacktop.

And that's when she saw it—their biggest clue yet!

Chapter Seven

"Look at that!" Andi cried as a bright red feather skittered across the ground. "It's just like the ones in Charlie's tail!" she said. She sprinted after the feather and caught it as it whirled into the air. Holding it tight, she darted back across the parking lot to her friends.

"Maybe he comes from a nearby house," Natalie suggested.

"Which direction is the wind blowing?" Tristan licked his index finger and raised it in the air, but it was impossible to tell.

"Can we scout around and see if we can find where the feather came from, Ms. McNicholas?" Natalie said.

Ms. McNicholas frowned. "I don't know . . ."

"Don't worry. We do this sort of thing all the time when we're looking for pets," Tristan said. "We won't take long."

"Okay. I'll wait in the car and keep an eye on you."

Andi jogged across the parking lot with Tristan and Natalie close behind her.

To the right of the hardware store was a car dealership. It was closed, so the Pet Finders peered in through the big windows. No empty parrot cage inside. "I don't think he came from here," Tristan said.

To the left of the home-improvement store was a community center—a modern brick building with a green roof. "Do town centers have parrots?" Andi asked doubtfully.

"Only one way to find out," Natalie said.

They headed toward it, through a small garden full of wind-tossed flowers. Suddenly, the main door opened and a group of well-dressed people streamed out, led by a photographer with an expensive-looking camera slung around his neck. "Let's have you all on the steps!" he said, throwing his arms wide. "That's it! Smaller people in front, tall ones behind."

The Pet Finders hesitated. They could hardly push through the crowd when they were having pictures taken.

"Uh-oh!" Andi said, catching sight of a woman in the center of the group. She was wearing a spectacular hat decorated with red feathers.

Natalie groaned.

"She could still be Charlie's owner," Tristan pointed out. "Maybe she saves Charlie's old feathers to decorate her hats."

"Not very likely, but let's go ask," Andi said as the photographer snapped the group shot.

"Excuse me," Natalie said to the woman in the feathery hat. "Have you lost a parrot?"

The woman looked surprised and shook her head, setting the feathers fluttering. She smiled suddenly. "Oh, you mean the hat? I didn't make it, darling, I bought it in town."

"Oh," Andi said, disappointed again. "Thanks."

The Pet Finders headed back to Ms. McNicholas's car. "Those feathers were too bright, anyway," Natalie admitted.

"And if all them had come out of Charlie's tail, he'd be bald!" Tristan added.

Andi couldn't help laughing. "We'll just have to work with the clues we have—all those weird things Charlie says and the charm around his leg."

"The trouble is, none of them make any sense," Natalie pointed out. "It's almost as frustrating as having no clues at all!"

*   *   *

Andi spent so much time over the weekend trying to solve the lost parrot case that she'd hardly spent a moment with Buddy. She raced home from school on Monday to work on his trick for the Pet Show. "Today's the day we're going to get this right, Bud," she said, taking the hoop into the backyard.

Buddy watched her with his head to one side.

"Come on, boy. Through you go."

The little terrier scampered up to the hoop, then flopped down on the grass beside it.

"You have to go through it." Andi took a dog treat out of her pocket and tossed it through the hoop. "Go on, boy!"

Buddy ran around the side of the hoop and wolfed down the treat.

"Oh, Buddy," Andi groaned.

Natalie appeared at the back door with Jet. "Hi, Andi. Your mom said you were out here. How's it going?"

Andi shrugged. "It's not."

Buddy ran off down the yard to play with his rubber bone. Jet loped after him.

"I don't know what to do next," Andi admitted. "I've tried throwing treats through the hoop, but he just cuts around the side to gobble them up."

"Why don't you *show* him how it's done?" Natalie

suggested. "Here, I'll hold the hoop and you jump through it."

Andi handed the hoop to Natalie then called Buddy. He trotted over, his tail wagging. Jet followed and settled down in a patch of sunshine.

"Come on, Bud. Pay attention." Andi commanded. She ran to the hoop, crouched down then hopped through awkwardly and glanced back to see what Buddy was doing.

He was watching her with his tongue hanging out.

"Come on, boy." Andi caught his collar and led him to the hoop. She jumped through again, pulling Buddy after her. "See? That's what you have to do!"

Letting go of his collar, Andi jumped through the hoop once more. To her delight, Buddy copied her. "He did it! Good boy, Bud! Good boy!" She hugged him. "Now, let's see you go by yourself."

Buddy scurried around the hoop and jumped through.

"Awesome!" Andi cried. "This calls for a celebration treat." She felt inside the pockets of her red hoodie. "Oops! I used all his treats."

"Let's go to Paws for Thought and buy some," Natalie suggested. "We can give the dogs a run in the park on the way."

* * *

The pet store was packed with people. "Look, there's Belle!" Andi said, recognizing the beautiful white husky she'd bathed at Aggie's grooming parlor. She ran her hands through the dog's soft, fluffy coat, and Belle cuddled her head against Andi's jeans.

Natalie stretched up on tiptoe. "Where's Tris? I thought he was supposed to be helping Christine today."

Andi scanned the store. She could just make out a mop of strawberry blond hair underneath a sign saying PET ENTRY FORMS. "There he is."

They wove their way through the crowd, admiring the well-groomed dogs they passed. Tristan was standing at a table on the far side of the store, handing out entry forms for the Pet Show.

"Hey, can you help me out?" He thrust a pile of forms at Andi. "Everyone wants to register for the Pet Show and I can't give these forms out fast enough."

"No problem," Andi said. She and Natalie helped hand out the forms and gradually the pet owners moved away from the table. Even so, the rest of the store was still crowded. There was at least a dozen people waiting in the checkout line alone.

When Christine finally finished ringing up orders, she came over to speak to them. "Wow! That was a rush. Poor Max is hiding out back."

"You and Fisher are doing an amazing job of organizing this show," Natalie said. "So many people are entering their pets."

"It's been great for business," Christine said. "And not only for my store. The hotels are booked all the way into Seattle, and restaurant reservations are soaring, too." She turned to Tristan. "I've got another job for you, if you're up for it."

"Sure he is," Natalie replied. "Tristan likes hard work, don't you, Tris?"

Tristan gave her a fake scowl. "Thanks a lot."

"Come on," Christine said. She led the kids into the stockroom. Two boxes brimming with papers sat on a low shelf. "These are all the show applications that came through the mail. We have to send everyone a program. Got it?"

"Yup." Tristan picked up one of the boxes. "We'll do it at the table in the store in case anyone else comes in for an entry form."

"We?" Natalie teased. "I don't remember volunteering to help you, Tris."

Tristan stared at her in dismay. "Come on, Nat. It'll take me forever to do it all by myself."

Andi laughed. "She's only kidding. Of course we'll help." She grabbed a pile of printed sheets and followed Tristan back to the table.

"Hey, here comes Amanda Singer," Natalie said, as they sat at the table in the shop. "I wonder if she's brought Windwhistle with her."

Mrs. Singer entered the store. Her little Chihuahua was in his pet carrier, peeping out through the grille. She set the box down, opened the door, and lifted Windwhistle out, putting him on the floor beside her. "You stretch your legs, darling. But stay close to me." She headed for the table where the Pet Finders were sitting.

"Well, you're very busy," she commented. "Do you work at Clip 'n' Curl *and* Paws for Thought?"

"We're helping out today because—" Tristan began.

Mrs. Singer didn't let him finish. "Has Windwhistle's herbal food supplement arrived yet?" she demanded.

"Sorry, I don't know," Tristan said. "Christine deals with special orders."

Christine came out of the storeroom. "Not in yet, I'm afraid, Amanda."

Andi noticed Buddy watching Windwhistle with interest as the tiny dog sniffed around the table. He trotted over to make friends, but when he sniffed Windwhistle, the Chihuahua gave a frightened yelp and dove into his pet carrier.

Buddy stared at him for a minute then flopped down beside Andi.

"Did the big dog scare you, my precious?" Mrs. Singer crooned. Windwhistle peered up at her, looking very anxious. She snapped the carrier shut and picked it up. "Don't worry. We're going home now," she said and marched out of the store.

"Poor Windwhistle," Andi said. "Buddy must have looked like a giant to him. But wasn't he sweet, peeping out of his carrier?"

"I don't think there's anything sweet about a dog that has to be carried around in an oversized purse!" Tristan exclaimed. "Why doesn't he walk, like every other dog?"

"Probably because he's so tiny," Andi said. "I guess everything must seem scary when you're no bigger than a slipper." She patted Buddy. "Though I can't imagine why he was afraid of you, Bud. You couldn't scare a fly."

Buddy licked her hand then turned his head to inspect the store.

"He's searching for a fly so he can prove you wrong," Tristan joked. "Now come on, let's start sending out these programs or we'll be here all night."

That evening, Andi's mom came home late from work. "What a day!" Mrs. Talbot sighed as she sank into an armchair. She took off her glasses and rubbed the bridge of her nose, then fluffed her short curly hair with both hands.

"Can I help with dinner?" Andi offered. She and her mom lived on their own. Andi's parents had divorced a year ago, and her dad lived in Arizona where he worked as an oil plant engineer. Luckily, her parents were still good friends and she got to see her dad during vacations and whenever he visted Seattle on business.

"Actually, I thought we'd go out tonight. We've both been so busy lately, it'd be nice to have a little girl time, right?"

Andi ran up to her room and changed to her favorite lilac top and a pair of black jeans with a neat purple belt. Her mom was waiting in the hall when she ran downstairs, and Buddy was sitting by the door, eyeing his leash hopefully. "Sorry. You can't come with us, Bud," Andi said, rubbing his chest. She hated to leave him alone. "We'll bring you back a great doggy bag, okay?"

Andi's mom took her to a nearby diner, which was warm, bright, and bustling. A waitress who wore her graying hair in a stiff, old-fashioned beehive showed them to a table near the counter. She handed them menus, then waited while they chose.

"I'll have a hamburger and french fries, please," Andi told her. "What are you having, Mom?"

"I'm not sure. I don't want anything too filling. In fact, what I'm really in the mood for is some breakfast."

"Breakfast at night?"

Mrs. Talbot laughed. "Call me crazy."

"You're crazy."

"All-day breakfasts are at the bottom of the menu," the waitress said, pointing to the list.

Mrs. Talbot scanned it quickly. "Two poached eggs on toast, please," she said.

"I think I'll have breakfast now, too," Andi said, checking the menu again. "I'd like to change to a bacon sandwich. With ketchup."

The waitress jotted the order in her notepad and walked away.

"You seem to be doing a great job with Buddy's training," said Mrs. Talbot.

"Thanks," Andi said. "I finally got him to jump through the hoop, but it took a lot of treats to get him there."

"And how's the parrot case?"

"Well, we put up posters and we have lots of clues, but—" Andi stopped abruptly as she heard the waitress call their order to the cook in the kitchen.

"Gimme a hammer slammer and paint it red! Adam and Eve on a raft!"

Chapter Eight

Hammer slammer! Paint it red! Adam and Eve on a raft! Andi almost fell off her chair. It was exactly what Charlie had been saying! Andi waved to the waitress. "Excuse me!"

The woman bustled back to their table. "Changed your mind again, did you?" she asked.

"No, but I heard you say Adam and Eve on a raft," Andi said. "What does that mean?"

The waitress laughed. "Oh, it's just a fun way to say two eggs on toast. Back in the day, we had lots of nicknames for orders."

"And hammer slammer?" Andi asked.

"Bacon sandwich," the woman told her. "Paint it red means with ketchup, of course."

"You haven't lost a parrot, have you?" Andi asked, her hopes soaring.

The waitress stared at Andi as though she had two heads. "A parrot? Uh, no. Is that a sandwich?"

"How about someone else who works here?" Andi persisted. "Does anyone here own a parrot?"

The waitress shook her head. "Sorry." A man at the far end of the diner had raised his hand to attract her attention. "Gotta go." She hurried away.

Andi's mom raised her eyebrows. "What was all that about?"

"Charlie keeps saying these weird things," Andi explained. "Like 'Adam and Eve on a raft,' and 'paint it red.' Parrots repeat things they hear, so there's a good chance he came from a diner."

"I'm impressed," Mrs. Talbot remarked.

"Now all I have to do is call all the diners in Orchard Park and find out which one lost a parrot."

"That's all, huh?" Mrs. Talbot smiled. "I think that'll have to wait until tomorrow. Here comes our dinner."

Andi turned to see the waitress heading their way with a tray of eggs and bacon. "You mean *breakfast*," she corrected.

Andi could hardly wait for lunchtime the next day. Ms. McNicholas had given the Pet Finders permission to borrow the phone book so they could call

Orchard Park diners and track down Charlie's owner.

Andi hopped onto Natalie's desk and flipped the directory to the right page. "There are tons of diners in the Seattle area, but only about ten in Orchard Park. We'll start with those and cross our fingers that Charlie didn't fly any farther, otherwise we could be calling diners forever."

"Another case almost solved!" Tristan cheered. "Thank goodness your mom took you out to eat last night!

"I should have realized Charlie was talking in diner slang," Ella said. "My aunt in Baltimore used to live next door to a diner, and she always calls coffee 'joe' because that's the diner slang name for it."

"Everyone knows *that* one," Natalie said irritably, but Ella was still talking.

"My mom and dad took me to a diner once that had the most amazing doughnuts," she went on. "They were shaped like stars and came in every flavor you could possibly think of. Raspberry, vanilla, cinnamon, blueberry—"

"Ella, we have to make these calls." Andi was afraid Ella's list of flavors might take up the whole lunch break.

"Oh, yeah, sure. I wish I'd brought my cell to school today. It's so cool and the latest model and—"

"You read out the numbers, Tris," Natalie said, ignoring Ella. "Andi and I will make the calls."

"I don't mind making some calls if someone will lend me their phone," Ella offered.

"No, thanks," Natalie snapped.

Tristan read out the first number on the list and Andi punched it into her phone. While it was ringing, Natalie dialed the number of the second diner on the list.

A man answered Andi's call: "Costa's Diner."

"Hi," Andi said. "My friends and I found a parrot. Have you lost one?"

"Huh?"

"A parrot," she repeated. "It knows diner slang, so we figured it comes from a diner."

"What is this? A prank phone call? Shouldn't you be in school?"

"No! Wait! I'm—" Andi tried to explain, but the man hung up. "I don't think Charlie came from Costa's," she told the others.

"No one's lost a parrot at the diner on Mill Road, either," Natalie said.

Andi punched in a new number, hoping for better luck.

But, to their disappointment, none of the Orchard Park diners had lost a parrot.

"That's that, then," Andi said, snapping her phone shut after she'd called the last place on the list. "Now what?"

"I have a horrible feeling we're going to have to call every diner in Seattle," Tristan said. He flipped over page after page of diner listings. "Twenty-three pages. It's going to take forever."

"But Charlie didn't seem tired when he flew through our window," Natalie pointed out. "Surely he'd have been worn out if he'd flown all the way from Seattle?"

"Well, maybe he stopped on the way to rest," said Tristan.

"Why don't we photocopy these pages and divide them up?" Ella suggested. "Then we can call from home."

"Or *three* of us can, anyway," Natalie muttered. "This is a Pet Finders case, after all."

But Ella didn't seem to hear. "I'll go ask Ms. McNicholas if we can use the copier in the office."

"I'll come with you." Tristan shrugged his shoulders at the other two girls and followed her out of the room.

Andi went to the window and gazed out. It was hard to stay focused when all their clues seemed to lead nowhere. Minutes ago she'd thought they were close to solving the case, but now it felt as though they were as far away from finding Charlie's owner as ever.

* * *

After an hour of calling diners after school, Andi was glad to help at the Clip 'n' Curl. It was crammed with customers when she arrived, and the phone was ringing nonstop. The waiting area was overflowing and people were standing in the salon with dogs of all shapes and sizes. There were even a few clients with cats that were eyeing the dogs nervously from inside their carriers.

"Am I glad to see you!" Aggie greeted her. "Natalie's just taken a beagle down to the kennels. Tristan isn't here yet, but I'm sure he'll be along in a minute. Would you run the bath, please, and start washing Spot? He's in the waiting room. Some of these people are waiting to pay, so I need to deal with them first."

"Sure." Andi went to the bath and turned on the water.

Joe was trying to groom a wriggling tan dachshund and Honey was sitting on Lena's table having her nails clipped. Andi went over to pet her. "I didn't expect to see her back so soon," she said, running her hand gently over Honey's fluffy head. "She was only here the other day."

"David thought her nails were getting a tiny bit too long and there won't be time to clip them on Saturday when she comes for her final wash and brushup before the show," Lena explained.

Andi went back to check the water level in the bath. As she squirted in a dollop of shampoo, she heard the door open and wondered if it was Tristan.

Mrs. Singer entered with Windwhistle in his pet carrier. "I need a new collar and leash for the show, Aggie," she called. "Be a dear and find me your very best, will you?"

"In a minute," Aggie replied. "When I've finished with the customers ahead of you."

Tristan arrived. "Any luck with the diners?" he asked Andi, swishing the bath water with his hand to make it bubblier.

"No. I'm going to try again . . ." She trailed off, realizing that Tristan was no longer listening. He was staring across the room, his face pink with excitement.

"See that, Andi?" he hissed, nodding to the other side of the salon. "That woman at the cash register has parrot pins all over her hat! *And* she's holding a pack of bird food with a picture of an African gray on it."

The woman finished paying and was walking out the door with her beautifully groomed Pekinese trotting beside her.

Tristan raced after her. "Wait!" As he ran, a red setter on an extendable leash bounded in front of him. The leash pulled taut and Tristan tripped over it, crashing to the floor and knocking over a display of fancy collars.

Pandemonium broke out. Dogs began barking and pulling on their leashes. Some broke free and began to tear through the salon, swerving around anyone who got in their way. Big dogs leaped over smaller ones. Leashes tangled. Owners yelled their dogs' names, trying to get them under control. Cats, still safe in their carriers, hissed and wailed furiously, adding to the commotion.

Andi quickly turned off the bath taps and ran to help Tristan, but she couldn't get through the chaos. She noticed a man with a dachshund enter the salon, gasp at the scene, and quickly exit, leaving the front door wide open.

Andi called to a man with a quivering Yorkie who was keeping cover behind the front counter. "Shut the door, please!" she cried. But he didn't move; he was too busy trying to calm his terrified dog. "Sir! The door!"

A German shepherd raced past her. She caught its leash and held on tight. "Who owns this one?" she shouted.

A woman grabbed the leash from her. "He's mine. Thanks."

Finally Andi reached Tristan, who was now on his feet. "You okay?" she asked.

"Nothing broken," he said, giving Andi an embarrassed grin. "But look what I did."

"Don't worry about it," Andi said. "Let's catch these dogs and give them back to their owners." She set off after a Great Dane.

Natalie came running in from the kennel and caught a yapping terrier by its collar. Aggie, Joe, and Lena were grabbing dogs, too. Before long, all the pets were rounded up and handed over to their owners.

"I'm really sorry, Aggie," Tristan apologized after he handed a half-brushed dachshund back to Joe.

"It was an accident. And no real harm's been done." Aggie righted a fallen laundry bin and stuffed the spilled wet towels back inside it.

Andi picked up a pin brush from the floor and rewound a reel of tangled ribbon.

"I'll go get the next dog," Natalie said. As she headed for the waiting area, David Nazrallah came into the shop.

"Hi there! I'm back for Honey. Is she all done?"

Andi glanced around, wondering who was looking after the tiny dog. In all the confusion, she hadn't even noticed her. But Aggie, Joe, and Lena were looking around as if they didn't know where Honey was either,

and she wasn't being held by anyone in the crowd of customers.

Andi thought hard. She last saw Honey perched on Lena's worktable having her nails clipped. Maybe she was hiding somewhere nearby. Trying to stay calm, she bent down and scanned the floor in all directions. There was no sign of her.

"Is something wrong?" asked David.

"Come out back, David," Aggie said, her face taut with anxiety. She led him through the purple velvet curtain.

"We've got to find Honey," Andi whispered to her friends.

They searched under tables, in laundry bins, in the towel cupboards, but there was no sign of her.

"Maybe she slipped into the waiting area to get away from all the noise," Natalie suggested.

"Has anyone seen a gold-and-white long-haired Chihuahua?" Tristan called as Andi led the way into the waiting area. "Ow!" he exclaimed when Natalie elbowed him.

"Keep it down!" she ordered.

Tristan asked the customers again, this time in a loud whisper.

"No, sorry," a woman replied. Everyone else shook their head.

"Let's try the kennels," Andi said.

They ran down the corridor, passing David and Aggie, who were clearly having a tense conversation. A cocker spaniel jumped up onto the door of his pen and barked as they raced into the kennels.

Andi threw open the door of an empty pen near the window. She could see that Honey wasn't in there, but maybe she was hiding under the quilt. She turned it over. Nothing.

Natalie and Tristan checked the other pens. Again, nothing.

"She's not in the salon . . . or the waiting room . . . or the kennel. . . ." Andi said in a shaky voice. "Honey's gone!"

Chapter Nine

Two police officers—a young woman with short brown hair and a rather stocky man with blond hair and a beard—arrived at the grooming parlor. David had called them immediately upon hearing the news.

"My show dog has been stolen," he explained. She's a long-haired Chihuahua." David was pale and Andi's heart went out to him. She'd felt exactly the same way when Buddy had disappeared during her first few days in Orchard Park.

Tristan sat on a stool in the corner of the salon with his head in his hands. "This is all my fault."

Andi slipped an arm around his shoulders, not knowing what to say.

"We'll need to take statements from everybody," the male officer said. "And it would be best to close the salon for the rest of the day. Has anybody left since the incident?"

"A few people," Aggie admitted.

"I can give you the names of everyone who was here." Lena flipped open the appointment book.

Aggie came over to the Pet Finders.

"I'm sorry, Aggie." Tristan shook his head. "If only I hadn't been running after that woman . . ." He trailed off.

"Listen, Tristan," she said, patting his arm. "You tripped over a leash. It was an accident. It could have happened to any one of us."

"Can I have another word with you, please, Ms. Patel?" the officer called.

Aggie went back to speak to him.

The clients who'd been waiting for their pets to be groomed gave their names to the second officer then left the salon, still exchanging whispers about what had happened.

"Where do you think Honey's gone?" Natalie asked Andi. "Do you think she really was *stolen*?"

"Maybe she ran outside. The door was open, and she's small enough to have darted out without anyone noticing."

Tristan sat up straighter on his stool. "Let's say she *was* stolen. Who would want to steal her?"

"Honey is a champion show dog," Andi pointed out.

"But what's the good of stealing a show dog if you can't put her in shows?" Natalie said. "Everyone would recognize her."

"Another show dog owner might want to take her," Tristan said slowly. "Especially if Honey was a big rival to her dog. Come on, you know this. We've seen this before."

Andi gasped. "Windwhistle! Amanda Singer was in here earlier."

"I'll find out where she lives," Tristan said, sounding determined. "I started all this, so it's up to me to sort it out."

"*Us*, you mean," Natalie reminded him. "You're not in this alone."

"Did I hear you say Honey had a rival?" asked the female officer, walking over.

"Windwhistle. He and Honey are favorites to win next Saturday's Pet Show," Natalie told her.

"Amanda Singer is Windwhistle's owner," Andi added. "She came into the salon just before the . . . uh . . . incident."

The officer added Mrs. Singer's name to the list of

customers. "We'll definitely need to interview her." She went to tell her partner.

"Mrs. Singer's our main suspect," Tristan said in a low voice. "But if the police are going to interview her, maybe we should start somewhere else."

Natalie frowned. "Where?"

"Outside," Andi said. "There's still a chance that Honey could have slipped out."

"I hope you're right," Tristan said. "A lost dog is easier to find than a stolen one."

The Pet Finders headed out of the salon to the sidewalk. "Where would a frightened Chihuahua hide?" Andi wondered, looking up and down the road.

"Somewhere she wouldn't get stepped on." Tristan crouched down to look under a parked car. "She's not here, but we should check all the cars."

They worked their way along the street, looking under every car. They couldn't think of anywhere else to look because the buildings were all right on the sidewalk, with no yards where a tiny dog could lose herself among the plants.

Soon they came to a narrow alley. At the far end they could see traffic rushing by on Main Street. "I hope she didn't go down there," Andi said.

"We should check it out," Tristan said. They trooped

down the alley and rushed out onto Main Street, startling a few shoppers.

"No sign of Honey," Andi said. "Let's try in the stores." The Pet Finders split up to ask some shop owners if they'd seen Honey, but no one had.

The kids searched until the stores closed then walked home slowly. "If she ran out of the salon, surely we'd have found her by now," Natalie said.

"It looks as though someone *must* have taken her," Andi admitted. "I know Amanda Singer is our main suspect, but we don't know where she lives, so we can't investigate her tonight. And there were a lot of other customers at Clip 'n' Curl who could have taken Honey."

"What about the lady with the parrot pins? Maybe that's why she didn't stop when I called," Tristan suggested.

"But that was before the commotion in the salon," Andi said. "Honey was still with Lena then, having her nails clipped."

"Oh, yeah," Tristan said. "So who else could have taken her? Someone with a bag, otherwise they'd have been seen carrying her outside, right?"

"I don't know," Natalie said. "She's so small. You said Honey could fit in a pocket when we first met her."

"I was only kidding. She's tiny, but not *that* tiny.

There's no way she'd fit in a pocket." Tristan kicked an empty can that lay on the sidewalk and sent it clattering along the road. "So who had a bag big enough to hold a Chihuahua?"

"Amanda Singer was carrying Windwhistle's pet carrier. I assumed Windwhistle was inside, but I didn't actually see him," Andi said. "Maybe she *brought* it empty so she could steal Honey."

"But how would she have known Honey was there?" Natalie asked.

Andi shrugged. "She could have been keeping watch and seen David take her in. Or maybe she had a peek at the appointment book. It wouldn't be hard—especially since Aggie, Joe, and Lena have been so busy."

"We have to check out Mrs. Singer's house," Tristan said.

"But we don't know her address," Natalie reminded him.

"We can ask at Clip 'n' Curl tomorrow," Andi said.

"Or we can stop by Paws for Thought and ask Christine," Tristan suggested. "Amanda's a customer, so she might have it."

Andi glanced at her watch and cried, "Shoot! I promised Mom I'd be in early tonight."

"I'm going to keep looking," Tristan called after her. "I'll call you if I find Honey."

The next day after school, the Pet Finders headed straight for Paws for Thought to see how Christine was doing with the Pet Show and to see if she had heard any news about Honey.

"Let's stop by Clip 'n' Curl, too," Natalie suggested. "Aggie might know how the police investigation's going."

"I can't show my face at the Clip 'n' Curl," Tristan said hurriedly. "Not after yesterday."

"What happened yesterday?" Ella asked from behind them.

Natalie put her hands on her hips. "Are you following us, Ella?"

Tristan blushed and quickly bent over to retie his sneaker lace. Andi could tell he was totally embarrassed.

"One of the dogs disappeared after a commotion," Andi said, shooting a warning glance at Natalie to stop her from blurting out Tristan's part in it.

"Whoa." Ella's eyes stretched wide. "We should look for her."

"We *have* been," Natalie said. "We're the Pet Finders. That's what we do. Come on, Tris." She tapped him with her foot. "Isn't that lace tied yet? We need to get a move on."

"Can I come along?" Ella asked.

"Sure!" Tristan piped up, much to Natalie's obvious dismay.

"Great! Are we going to be investigating the missing Chihuahua? I'm really good at finding stuff. I once found my mom's wedding ring that had been lost for days. It was . . ."

"This is all we need," Natalie mumbled to Andi.

When they reached Paws for Thought, Ella stopped outside. "Look at this!" she exclaimed. "The owner of this store must be the thief!"

"Of course she's not!" Natalie snapped. "Christine is our friend."

"But she's got a card in her window advertising a long-haired Chihuahua for sale. She's probably got the dog locked in a back room somewhere," Ella speculated.

"I'm not sure the thief would be that obvious about selling Honey," Andi said gently. "I mean, if you'd stolen a valuable show dog, you wouldn't advertise the fact."

"Even if it wasn't Christine who wrote out the card," Ella said, "we should still ask who posted it. It could be a clue."

"She does have a point," Tristan admitted.

Andi had to agree. "Okay. Let's check it out."

Inside the shop, Christine was on the phone and Max was lying in his usual spot in the window display, between a cat bed and an arrangement of leashes. He jumped down to see them, his tail wagging. Andi found a dog treat in her pocket for him. Then he ambled back to the window and squeezed past a display of dog food tins before flopping down again.

Ella was over by the counter talking to Christine, who had finished her phone conversation. "Scott Carling, a reputable Chihuahua breeder, put up that poster," Christine was saying. "There's no way he'd be mixed up in Honey's disappearance. He's a good friend of mine."

Natalie nudged Andi. "Why doesn't Ella keep out of this? She has no right to accuse Christine of anything."

Tristan sprang to Ella's defense. "She just wants to help."

Natalie didn't say any more, but Andi could tell she was almost at the end of her patience. Andi bit her lip, hoping Natalie wouldn't lose her temper. She wasn't exactly famous for being diplomatic! "Is there any news of Honey, Christine?" she asked, going over to the counter.

"No. I spoke to Aggie earlier. David Nazrallah's very upset, understandably. To be honest, the whole thing is turning into a disaster—not just for David and Honey, but for the Pet Show, too. I've had several calls today from people who want to cancel their entries. They won't risk bringing their pets here if there's a dog thief in the area." She sighed and ran a hand through her dark hair. "We were relying on some top names from the dog show world to pull in the crowds and put the Orchard Park show on the map. Unfortunately some of the show categories will have to be canceled if things go on like this."

"How did everyone find out so quickly?" Andi asked.

"Amanda Singer's been telling them, apparently," Christine replied. "And it made today's local paper, too." She showed them the article, with a photo of David standing sadly beside Honey's empty dog basket.

"I bet Mrs. Singer's trying to guarantee a win for Windwhistle by knocking out the competition," Natalie said.

"She won't have a class for her precious pooch to compete in if everyone cancels," Tristan pointed out.

"But we should definitely go see her. Do you know her address, Christine?"

"Yes, but I don't want you making a nuisance of yourselves."

"Us? A nuisance?" Tristan protested innocently.

Christine laughed, the worry lines disappearing from her face for a moment. "It's been known to happen. But I guess you know what you're doing when it comes to missing pets. And besides, you can save me a trip. I've got that herbal diet supplement to deliver to her."

"Perfect!" Natalie exclaimed. "Let's get over there right away. Her little poppet will need his vitamins!"

Chapter Ten

"Let's pick up Buddy and Jet on the way to Mrs. Singer's house," Andi suggested. "They'll like the exercise and having them with us will show Mrs. Singer that we're dog lovers, too. Maybe she'll let us come in and play with Windwhistle."

"Doubtful," added Nat.

"Hey, guys, I wish I could come, but I have to finish a history project," Ella said. "See you later!" She turned and headed in the opposite direction.

"She must love studying," Tristan remarked. "Our project's not due until next week."

Buddy and Jet were thrilled to be along for the walk to Amanda Singer's house. They bounded around each other so energetically that their leashes got tangled and the Pet Finders had to keep stopping to pry them apart.

Amanda Singer lived in a modern, flat-roofed house set behind a high wall. "Whoa!" Natalie marveled as they went in through the fancy iron gate. The front wall of the house was made entirely of mirrored glass, which reflected a spectacular fountain in the middle of the front yard.

As they drew nearer, Natalie checked herself out in one of the windows. She smoothed her jacket and tucked a strand of blond hair behind one ear.

The main entrance was at the side of the building, along a narrow path of violet-gray slate chips. Mrs. Singer answered their knock.

"We've brought Windwhistle's herbal diet supplement from Paws for Thought," Andi said. She handed the packet over, and then moved to one side so she could see past Mrs. Singer into the house.

"Thank you." Mrs. Singer moved slightly, blocking Andi's view. She looked as though she was about to close the door.

"Nice house," Tristan jumped in. "Have you ever thought of selling? My parents are in the real estate business."

"Thanks, but we like it here. My husband and I had it built to our own design three years ago. Now, if there's nothing else—"

"Can we see Windwhistle?" Natalie said hurriedly. "We really love dogs."

"I'm afraid not," Mrs. Singer said.

That's suspicious, Andi thought. *Why would she stop us from coming in if she has nothing to hide?*

"Some dogs try to pick fights, and he is far too small to defend himself," Mrs. Singer added.

"I don't mind waiting out here with the dogs," Natalie volunteered.

"Oh. Well, in that case . . . " Mrs. Singer opened the door wide.

Andi handed Buddy's leash to Natalie and followed Tristan inside.

The main room of the house was huge. They could see a gleaming, professional-style kitchen with brushed steel counters beyond the three creamy leather sofas arranged around a low table made from a big slab of tree trunk. To Andi's disappointment, there was no sign of Honey.

Mrs. Singer ushered them into a smaller but equally luxurious room. "This is Windwhistle's room," she said.

Tristan raised his eyebrows and shot Andi a look that said very plainly that giving a dog its own room was taking things *way* too far. Luckily, Mrs. Singer didn't notice.

Windwhistle was lying on a low couch covered with a thick sheepskin rug. On the wall behind him were shelves and shelves of dog toys, feeding bowls, and collars and leashes in every color of the rainbow. His white pet carrier stood in the corner, but Andi could see right inside it and Honey wasn't there.

The dog sat up and looked them over. Then he jumped down and trotted to greet them, lifting his feet daintily and wagging his fluffy tail.

"He's very cute," Andi said, kneeling on the deep, pale blue carpet to pet him. Windwhistle rolled over so she could rub his tummy. His fur felt as soft as down feathers. "Aren't you lucky, having all these fabulous toys?" she told him.

"Nothing but the best for my little poppet," Mrs. Singer said proudly.

Tristan sidled over to the couch and casually lifted the rug to check that Honey wasn't hidden in its folds.

"What are you doing?" Mrs. Singer asked, her eyes narrowing.

"I . . . um . . . I was just checking out how soft this rug is. Windwhistle must love it."

"Yes." Mrs. Singer relaxed. "It's his favorite place to nap."

"My dog likes lying on my bed," Andi said, wondering if they could find an excuse for going upstairs.

"Windwhistle spends a lot of time upstairs," Mrs. Singer said. "Especially if I have to go out without him. But this room is his pride and joy. He always comes in here when I'm cooking so he can be near me. I don't allow him in the kitchen area—not since a horrible accident with tomato sauce."

Tristan came to kneel beside Andi. He rubbed Windwhistle's chest gently. "It's terrible about poor Honey disappearing like that, isn't it?" he said, trying to turn the conversation.

"Oh, it is," agreed Mrs. Singer. "I'm so worried that Windwhistle might vanish next. Perhaps the thief is targeting Chihuahuas. I've had extra locks fitted on all my windows, and I've got the police station's number next to my phone so I can contact them immediately if anything happens."

"That should keep him safe," Tristan said. He leaned close to Andi and whispered, "I have a feeling she didn't take Honey. It's another dead end."

"If we could only check out the upstairs, too," Andi replied quietly. "Just so we can be sure Honey's not here." She raised her voice. "You have a beautiful house, Mrs. Singer."

"Would you like to see the rest of it?" she asked, to Andi's relief. "It was featured in an issue of *Abode*, and the master suite won their Best Bedroom Award."

"That would be great," Andi said honestly.

Mrs. Singer led them across the main room and up a glass staircase. There were three bedrooms, all decorated in varying shades of blue, with deep carpets and mounds of silk cushions on the beds.

"Honey's definitely not here," Andi whispered when they had seen all the rooms. Apart from two portraits of Windwhistle—one at the top of the stairs and one in the master bedroom—there was nothing doggy upstairs at all. Every window had a lock fitted, too. A large sheet of paper with a phone number and the words POLICE STATION written on it was taped to the wall by the phone in the master bedroom. It looked as though Mrs. Singer had been telling the truth when she'd said she was afraid that Windwhistle might be stolen, too.

"Thank you for showing us your house and for letting us see Windwhistle," Andi said as they walked to the front door.

"You're very welcome! Come again if you like," she said as she let them out.

Natalie listened eagerly while they told her everything they'd found out.

"I'm sure she's not involved," Tristan said. "She must have put in those window locks to protect Windwhistle like she said—I had a look at them, and they're very shiny and new."

"We're getting nowhere fast," Natalie sighed. "We don't even know for sure whether Honey is lost or stolen. If she ran out of the salon on her own, why didn't we find her when we searched the area? She'd only been missing for about twenty minutes, so she couldn't have gone far."

"And if she *has* been stolen," Tristan said, "then who took her? We've eliminated our only suspect."

"We'll have to come up with a new lead," Andi said. "And we'd better do it soon, or Honey won't be back in time for the Pet Show."

When Andi arrived home her mom came out to the hall to meet her. "Great news, Andi! Your parrot's owner called. She saw your posters. She says the bird's name is Bertie."

"That's awesome!" Andi whooped. "Did she say how Bertie got out?"

"Well, the owner just moved to Orchard Park. One of the moving guys knocked over the parrot cage. The cage door opened, and Bertie flew away. His owner's name is

Claire Snowdon, and she's coming to your school in the morning to pick him up."

Andi was thrilled. At least they'd managed to solve one of their cases, and now they'd have more time for finding Honey. And with the way things were going, the Pet Finders Club was going to need all the spare hours they could get!

Andi, Natalie, and Tristan arrived at school a little early the next morning. They wanted to say a last good-bye to Charlie before Ms. Snowdon came to collect him.

"You're going home, Charlie," Andi said, reaching through the bars of the cage to stroke the parrot's soft chest feathers.

The classroom door opened and Ms. McNicholas came in. She was followed by a woman with long brown hair who wore a hand-knitted sweater over her paint-stained jeans.

"I'll be sorry to see Charlie go," Natalie said, watching Ms. Snowdon's face break into a smile when she saw the parrot.

"Me, too. But not as sorry as Ms. McNicholas," Tristan added. The teacher's eyes looked a little wet.

"It'll be good for Charlie to go home, though," Andi reminded them.

"These are the children who made the posters about Charlie . . . I mean, Bertie." Ms. McNicholas motioned for them to come over to meet Ms. Snowdon.

"Thank you," said Ms. Snowdon. "I don't know how I would have found Bertie if it hadn't been for you."

"That's okay," Andi said. She looked at Ms. Snowdon's jeans. "I guess you've been decorating."

"Yes. We've . . . um . . . just moved here."

"You don't seem to have any spots of red paint, though," Natalie said lightly. "Didn't you want to take Bertie's advice?"

"Advice?" Ms. Snowdon stared at Natalie as if she were from another planet. "What do you mean, advice?"

"To paint it red," Natalie said.

Ms. Snowdon looked baffled.

"It's one of the things Bertie says," Tristan added.

Andi began to feel uneasy. Surely Ms. Snowdon must have heard her parrot speaking.

At that moment, Bertie spread his wings inside his cage. "*Aak!* Adam and Eve on a raft!" he squawked.

Ms. Snowdon nearly jumped out of her skin.

The Pet Finders exchanged suspicious glances. "Do you think she's really his owner?" Andi whispered, drawing Natalie and Tristan aside.

"That's just what I was wondering," Natalie replied in a low voice. "Parrots are pretty valuable. Maybe she made up her mind to steal him after she saw the posters."

"Adam and Eve on a raft!" the parrot cried again.

"I guess you do a lot of rafting," Andi said to Ms. Snowdon.

"Rafting?" Ms. Snowdon gave a nervous laugh. "Oh, yes. I'm always out on the water. I take the bird with me. He loves that raft!"

Andi's doubts about the owner grew. She knew "Adam and Eve on a raft" meant two eggs on toast. It had nothing to do with rafting.

"Would you mind just describing the charm on the parrot's leg?" Andi asked. "You know, as a security check before you take him home." She was suddenly glad that Natalie's cell phone photo of the parrot had been a little blurry. Only someone who really knew the parrot would be able to describe the palm tree.

Tristan stepped in front of the cage so Ms. Snowdon could not see the bird.

The color drained from Ms. Snowdon's face. "A charm. Yes, of course. It's . . . um . . . gold. Well, a sort of silvery-goldy color."

"And what shape is it?" Natalie prompted.

Ms. McNicholas was staring at the Pet Finders in open-mouthed surprise, but she didn't say anything to stop them.

"Well, I . . ." Looking flustered, Ms. Snowdon peered over Tristan's shoulder toward the parrot cage, but Andi knew she was too far away to see the charm clearly. "I'm sorry, I appear to have made a mistake," the woman said suddenly. "It must not be my parrot, after all." She turned and ran out of the door, barging past Ms. McNicholas in her haste to get away.

"Thank goodness you were in the classroom." Ms. McNicholas hurried to the cage to stroke the parrot. "I'd have just handed Charlie over to Ms. Snowdon without checking a thing. Who knows what would have happened to him!"

"We had a case a bit like this a while back," Andi told her, "when someone called asking for payment in return for a lost dog. He didn't have the dog at all—he just wanted the owners to mail him a reward."

The bell rang for the start of school. "I'll just run down to the office and call Fisher," Ms. McNicholas said. "He needs to know that a would-be parrot thief is in the area." She hurried out of the classroom.

"I'd better go, too," Tristan said.

Andi and Natalie headed to their seats. "It was lucky

we spotted Ms. Snowdon's scam," Natalie said, "but poor Charlie still doesn't have a real owner."

"Yeah, but at least Charlie has a nice cage to live in," Andi said. "Poor little Honey could be anywhere!"

After school, the Pet Finders rushed back to Andi's house to make posters for Honey. Andi typed HELP HONEY! at the top of the page in large letters. Underneath it she added, Lost: Long-haired Chihuahua. They found a photo of the tiny dog on David Nazrallah's website and pasted it onto the poster, then added Andi's phone number.

"If she *is* lost, these should do the trick," Andi said as the posters spooled out of the printer. "Honey is so eye-catching, she must have been spotted by someone." She sighed. "The posters won't be much help if someone stole her, though."

As soon as the posters were printed, the Pet Finders sped down to Main Street and began taping them to lampposts and parking signs. They searched for Honey as they went along, calling her name, peering under parked cars and behind tubs of flowers, and scouting down the narrow alleys that ran beside the shops. Andi felt her stomach tightening anxiously with every step they took. Honey was so tiny. How could she survive out here with no one to look after her?

The sky darkened and a pale moon appeared. "We're going to have to give up for tonight," Tristan said glumly. "We'll never find her in the dark."

Natalie sighed. "Poor Honey will have to spend another night outside—unless a dognapper's got her."

Andi shivered. She couldn't decide which was worse.

As they headed back the way they'd come, they heard footsteps pounding toward them from behind. Turning, they saw Hannah Ling. Hannah's mom, Amy, ran the deli next to Paws for Thought.

"Wait!" Hannah said, panting. She grabbed Andi's sleeve.

"What's up?" Andi asked.

"That missing dog!" Hannah said in a rush. "The one on your posters. It's in our backyard!"

Chapter Eleven

The Pet Finders charged along Main Street after Hannah, dashed into the deli's side alley, and arrived in the backyard breathless. Hannah's mom was standing at the back door shining a flashlight on a pile of empty cardboard boxes. "She's still in there," Mrs. Ling said in a low voice. "One of the boxes just moved." She handed the flashlight to Tristan. "Be careful."

"It's okay," Tristan replied. "I know it's not safe to rush up to a strange dog, but Honey should recognize me."

The Pet Finders tiptoed toward the boxes. "Honey!" Andi called. "Here, girl."

The beam picked up a patch of tan fur. "I think I see her," Natalie whispered.

The tiny dog shrank down behind a box.

"It's okay, Honey," Andi reassured her. "We've come

to help you." She leaned forward and shifted the box a little. "Shine the light closer, Tris."

Tristan held the flashlight higher. Andi and Natalie took a peek behind the box and gasped.

"What's wrong?" Hannah cried.

"It's not Honey. It's a tan puppy," Natalie said, her voice heavy with disappointment.

Then a deep growl sounded behind them.

Andi whirled around and saw a large fierce-looking dog standing in the gateway to the alley. She gulped.

"It's the same color as the pup," Tristan whispered. "It must be the mother."

"We have to get out of her way," Andi whispered back. "She probably thinks we'll hurt her baby." The Pet Finders backed away from the dog and her puppy, edging slowly toward the deli so that the dog wouldn't think they were a threat.

The mother gave another growl and padded past them to pick up the puppy. She gently gripped the scruff of its neck in her teeth and trotted out of the yard.

"She's so thin," Tristan said. "She must be a stray. Come on, we have to follow her so Fisher can get her. She needs someone to help her and her puppy."

The Pet Finders and Hannah tracked the dogs from a safe distance.

"I'll call Fisher," Natalie said, pulling out her cell phone.

The dog trotted along Main Street with the puppy dangling from her mouth. Then she turned onto a quiet side street. As Andi and her friends reached the corner, they saw the dog slip between a Dumpster and a high wall.

"What's she doing?" Tristan wondered, shining the flashlight toward the gap. The beam of light showed a shadowy space littered with rubbish. A rusty shopping cart lay on its side amid tattered sheets of newspaper, dented drink cans, and empty bottles. The dog settled her puppy inside the shopping cart.

"She's got three other pups in there already!" Andi stood on tiptoe to get a better view. "Oh, they're so cute!"

"Fisher's on his way," Natalie said, flipping her phone shut and coming to stand by Andi so she could see the pups, too.

"This is so exciting!" Hannah said, staring so hard at the family of dogs that she could have been under a binding spell. "Pet finding is awesome!"

"It is," Andi agreed. "Or it is when it works out, anyway." Though she was glad to think that they were helping this poor stray dog and her puppies, she couldn't forget the fact that Honey was still missing.

The Pet Finders kept watch while they waited for Fisher. They didn't want the dog to run off with her puppies when help was on its way, although they knew they couldn't stop her if she decided to move. It could be dangerous to approach a strange dog, especially when it could have had bad experiences with people.

After about ten minutes, the ASPCA van turned into the alley, its headlights illuminating the buildings and the Dumpster. Andi blinked and raised her hand to shield her eyes.

Fisher parked next to the Dumpster. "Where are they?" he asked as he climbed out. He was holding a dog-catching pole with a noose at one end.

"Right behind there," Tristan said, pointing to the Dumpster.

"You four stay back," Fisher warned. He took a bowl of dog food from the passenger seat of the van and placed it close to the Dumpster. "Here, girl," he called softly. Then he stood back and waited to see what would happen.

Andi held her breath as the dog emerged from behind the Dumpster and cautiously approached the bowl. As soon as she reached the food she started to wolf it down.

"Poor thing," Fisher commented. "She's starving." He

took a step toward the dog, holding out the pole. "Good girl. You eat up."

The dog jumped back and Fisher froze.

After eyeing him nervously for a few seconds, she slowly moved back to the bowl for another mouthful.

"That's it, girl," Fisher said, inching toward her again.

The dog stopped eating and watched him again, but this time she didn't back away.

Fisher crept forward until he was close enough to use the dog-catching device. Slowly lowering the pole, he slipped the noose over the dog's head. When she realized what had happened, she tried to run off, but the noose tightened around her neck until it was as snug as a regular collar. "Good girl," Fisher said calmly. "Don't worry, you're safe now." He led her toward the van.

The dog struggled to break free, but Fisher held tight to the pole and guided her into the traveling cage.

"You stay there while I fetch your pups," he said, loosening the noose and slipping it off. He quickly shut the cage door to prevent her from escaping.

The dog howled pitifully as Fisher squeezed behind the Dumpster. He emerged a few seconds later with two puppies cradled against his chest. They were thin and dirty, and even from this distance Andi could see that they were shivering. "I think we found them just in

time," she said to Hannah. "Thank goodness you spotted that puppy."

"I went to look for Honey out in my yard because I saw your poster." Hannah explained as Fisher carried the puppies to the van. "I really thought I'd found her!"

The dog stopped howling when she saw her pups. She watched anxiously as Fisher placed them in the next traveling cage, then lay down with her nose against the bars that separated her from her babies.

Fisher returned to the shopping cart and brought out the last two pups and put them with the rest. "You guys did a great job," he said when he'd finished tucking them all in together. "We'll keep them at the center until they're stronger, then we'll find them homes. They're so cute, I don't think we'll have any problem placing them." He climbed into the driver's seat of the van. "See you!"

The Pet Finders and Hannah returned to the deli to make sure there were no more puppies around. "Look," Andi said as they poked through the boxes. "Here's an old blanket. This must be where the dog had her babies."

"I wonder why she decided to move them," Tristan mused.

"We're having a new storeroom built," Hannah said.

"My dad's been shifting stuff in the backyard all day to make space for it. I guess the mama dog thought it wasn't a safe place for her babies anymore."

"It's been a really exciting evening," Natalie said. "The only thing is, it hasn't brought us any closer to finding poor Honey."

On Friday, the Pet Finders and Ella met up in the school-yard during morning recess. It was dotted with puddles that reflected the dull gray sky. "The Pet Show is tomorrow," Tristan said, turning up his collar against the cold wind, "and we haven't found Honey yet." They'd searched every street within two miles of Clip 'n' Curl and put up at least fifty posters, but the Chihuahua seemed to have vanished into thin air.

"I stopped by Clip 'n' Curl yesterday," Natalie said. "I thought it was worth checking out the appointment book for the day that Honey disappeared."

"Did you find out anything useful?" Andi asked. She'd intended to go to the grooming salon herself, but keeping up with all the homework Ms. McNicholas was dishing out *and* trying to teach Buddy his trick had meant she'd had hardly a moment of free time.

Natalie shook her head. "There were tons of appointments that day, but we already knew that. And none of the customers seem suspicious. Aggie knows most of them and she's sure they wouldn't have stolen Honey. The only ones she hadn't seen before were an old lady who's nearly blind—she brought a pug that was so fat it could hardly walk, Aggie said—and an eight-year-old girl with an enormous crossbreed."

Tristan sighed. "Neither of them sounds like a dog-napper."

"What if Aggie stole Honey herself?" Ella said. "Or maybe it was someone else who works in the salon. Maybe one of them has always wanted a dog of their own and can't afford to buy one."

"Aggie, Lena, and Joe wouldn't steal a dog," Natalie snapped. "You should get your facts straight before you start accusing people, Ella. Christine was really upset when you—"

"Ella's only trying to help," Andi said, shooting Natalie a warning look. It was going to take a team effort—including Ella's help—to solve both cases.

"We haven't found Charlie's owners, either," Tristan pointed out as if he had read Andi's mind. They'd stopped working through the diner lists when Ms. Snowdon called Andi's mom. The delay meant they still had lots of diners to call.

"Maybe we could concentrate on calling places that

have a tropical name," Andi suggested. "To tie in with Charlie's palm-tree charm."

"Great idea!" Ella exclaimed. "Anywhere with 'Caribbean' or 'island' in the name would be a good place to start. Did I ever tell you about the vacation I had in the Caribbean?"

Just then, a rainbow-colored van pulled up outside the school.

"What's Jango doing here?" Tristan wondered.

They watched as Jango Pearce climbed out of his van, opened the back door, and took out several large boxes.

"Looks like he's brought you a little snack, Tris," Natalie teased.

"I wish," Tristan said. "Let's go and see what he's up to."

"Hi, Jango!" Andi called.

"Ho, there," he called back. His gray hair stood on end, and he looked a little flustered. "I'm running late today because some checkout guy at the wholesale warehouse kept asking if I'd found my parrot."

"You've lost Long John Silver?" Andi asked, shocked.

"No way! He's marching up and down my counter just the same as ever. I kept telling the guy it wasn't my parrot that was missing, but he wouldn't listen."

The Pet Finders looked at one another. "Maybe he

heard about another customer losing a parrot and thought it was you," Natalie guessed. "Everyone in town knows you've got a parrot."

"There must be other cafés with parrots," Jango grumbled. "Why doesn't the checkout guy pester *their* owners?"

"Hey, that's right!" Tristan exclaimed. "If Charlie's owner runs a diner, then he or she has to buy stock from a wholesale warehouse. Maybe it's the same warehouse that Jango uses." He clutched Andi's arm. "We've got to go there."

"Where's the warehouse, Jango?" asked Andi.

"On the highway about half a mile out of town. Now, let me get these brownies to your cafeteria. See you."

"Bye, Jango," the kids chorused.

"We have to tell Ms. McNicholas about this new lead," Andi said. "Come on!"

At lunchtime, the Pet Finders piled into Ms. McNicholas's sports car for the trip to the wholesale warehouse. The teacher had asked the principal for permission to take them out of school for an hour. There was no room for Ella in the car, but she didn't seem to mind. "Tell me all about it when you get back," she called as Ms.

McNicholas started the engine. "And I'll finish telling you about my Caribbean vacation!"

"How come you're in the front again, Tristan?" Natalie complained as they sped through town. "It should be your turn to be squashed up in the back with Andi."

"Or with *you*," Andi told Natalie. "I haven't had a turn in the front yet, either."

"I'm saving you two from having an argument about who gets to sit here," Tristan said, settling more comfortably into the seat.

Natalie swiped at the back of his head and Andi laughed. The gloom she'd felt earlier had vanished as soon as Jango had given them this new lead.

Ms. McNicholas pulled up in front of the wholesale warehouse, and they all piled out of the car and into the building. The place was quiet and the checkout man was reading a newspaper.

"Can we ask you about a lost parrot, please?" Andi began.

The man looked up. He was heavily built with folds of skin around his chin and neck and reminded Andi of a bloodhound. "Not another one!" he said, laying down the newspaper. "Everyone's losing parrots these days."

"Actually, we've found one," Natalie said. "Jango

Pearce said you'd mentioned someone who lost one."

"Yeah. Maureen, the other cashier, was telling me about it," the man said. "I thought it was Jango's, but I was wrong."

"Is that Maureen?" Andi asked, pointing to a red-haired woman at the next counter.

"That's right. Hey, Maureen," he called. "These kids are asking about that missing parrot."

"We found one, actually," Tristan told her.

The woman came over, pushing her eyeglasses up and into her hair. "A customer lost one a couple of weeks ago—the pineapple lady. I call her that because she bought so many pineapples. A hundred cases. Cleared us right out."

"Do you know her real name and address?" Andi asked the cashier.

"No, sorry. She had her own van, so we didn't have to deliver. And she's not a regular. I'd never seen her before."

"Oh, no," Natalie groaned. "I really thought we were getting somewhere."

"We still are," Tristan said. "She bought loads of pineapples. That's got to be a clue, right?"

"Uh-huh." Andi nodded. "And we're almost positive that Charlie comes from a diner."

"But a diner that serves tons of pineapples?" Natalie asked, confused.

"Why not? The Banana Café serves tons of bananas. So, maybe Charlie's diner has lots of pineapple specials!"

"Plus, pineapples are exotic, so they tie in with the palm tree charm on Charlie's leg. Maybe the diner's even got an exotic name."

Andi did a little skip, feeling that this time they really *were* on to something. She took out the list of diners she'd been calling. They'd divided the list alphabetically and Andi had the final third, from R to Z. So far, she'd only got up to V. Hurriedly she scanned the list.

"Here!" she cried, stabbing the last name with her finger. "Zebedee's Pineapple Paradise. This has to be our parrot's home. It just has to!"

Chapter Twelve

The Pet Finders tried to call the Pineapple Paradise diner several times before giving up completely. No one answered.

"Maybe they're slammed with business. All the time. Hammer Slammer!" Tristan exclaimed.

"Clever," Natalie groaned.

The kids were disappointed to hear that Ms. McNicholas wouldn't let them miss more school that day so that they could try to return Charlie to his home right away. But at least she agreed to drive them to Zebedee's Pineapple Paradise later, after school.

The afternoon seemed to crawl by. Andi found herself constantly glancing at the clock, but the hands seemed to be stuck in one place. At the end of the day, she and Natalie packed their backpacks then raced to the teacher's desk. "Are you ready, Ms. McNicholas?"

"Yes. Go get Tristan, please," she said.

Andi and Natalie flew to the door, intending to run to his classroom, but he was already waiting for them in the corridor, hopping from foot to foot.

Ms. McNicholas picked up Charlie's cage and carried it out to the car, with the Pet Finders close behind. "I'll hold him on my lap while you drive, okay, Ms. McNicholas?" Tristan said.

"Thank you, Tristan," Ms. McNicholas replied, handing him the cage and taking out her car keys.

Tristan grinned at Andi and Natalie. "Looks like I'm in the front again. There's no room in the back for two people and a parrot cage."

Natalie fumed.

It didn't take long to cross Orchard Park, and they were soon pulling into the Zebedee's parking lot right on the edge of town.

"Look at the sign!" Natalie exclaimed. It was shaped like a palm tree—exactly like the charm on their parrot's leg.

Charlie began to squawk and flap his wings.

"I think he knows he's home," Andi said.

Ms. McNicholas got out of the car and came around to the passenger door and opened it. She looked as though she was fighting back tears as she took the cage from

Tristan. Andi realized that the teacher was going to find it hard to say good-bye to the friendly bird.

"Oh, no!" Tristan groaned. "I'm covered in parrot seed. And I'm wet. Charlie's water must have spilled." He climbed out of the car and began to brush his jeans.

Natalie hooted with laughter. "What a shame!" She winked at Andi. "Maybe you should have let one of us sit up front with the cage. That way you wouldn't look like a birdfeeder right now."

They crossed the parking lot and went into the diner, a large crowded room with a tropical island mural painted on the far wall. Every table held parrot-shaped salt-and-pepper shakers and there were two fake palm trees near the door. A large empty parrot cage stood on the far end of the polished counter that ran nearly the length of the diner. Charlie squawked louder than ever and a woman came running out of the kitchen carrying a tray of pineapple slices.

"Zebedee!" she cried, her face lighting up. She dashed over and took the cage from Ms. McNicholas. "Where have you been, you naughty boy?"

"He flew into our classroom at school," Andi explained. "But luckily Ms. McNicholas, our teacher, knows all about parrots, so we've been looking after him while we tried to find you."

"These guys have worked really hard to track you down," Ms. McNicholas added.

"Oh, thank you!" said the woman. "I thought I'd never see him again."

She lifted the parrot out of the cage and let him walk up her arm and onto her shoulder, where he nuzzled her ear. "It's so great to have him home," she said, stroking his feathers. "If you stay here for a moment, I'll put Zebedee back in his cage, then I'll find you a table." She walked to the cage, but the parrot didn't want to go inside. Instead, he hopped up onto her head.

"Come on, boy," she said, reaching up to fetch him. "You can't fly around loose while the diner's open. Some customers might not take too kindly to a parrot visiting their table. And I don't want you flying away again."

"Adam and Eve on a raft!" the parrot squawked as his owner shut him in his cage.

"I'm not surprised that you solve so many missing pet cases," Ms. McNicholas said, smiling at the Pet Finders. "You should all be proud of yourselves."

Andi felt herself blush.

Zebedee's owner came back with four pineapple-shaped menus. "I'm Krista DeJoseph, and you've just made me the happiest woman in the world. Order whatever you want. It's on the house!"

They sat at the table nearest the parrot's cage and watched him jumping from perch to perch as he got to know his old home again.

Andi opened her menu. "Hey, look. All Charlie's—I mean, Zebedee's—phrases are here. A Short Lumberjack is three pancakes and a tall one's a stack of six."

"An Italian Scallion is salami, ham, provolone cheese, roasted peppers, and scallions on a hero," Tristan said.

"Here's a Hammer Slammer, too," added Ms. McNicholas. "And Adam and Eve on a Raft."

Krista came back to take their orders.

"I'll have a hamburger with lettuce and onions, please," Andi said.

"Gimme one hockey puck, take it through the garden, and pin a rose on it," Krista shouted to the chef.

"Paint it red! *Aak!*" Zebedee squawked.

Andi laughed. "How did he know I wanted ketchup on it?"

"Can I get you a pineapple juice, too?" Krista asked. "It's fresh squeezed. The best pineapple juice in the USA!"

"I'm really happy for Krista," Ms. McNicholas said while they waited for the food to come, "but I'm going to miss having a parrot."

"Why don't you get a bird of your own?" Tristan suggested.

Ms. McNicholas looked thoughtful. "Maybe I will."

"It's good to have a pet," Andi said encouragingly.
This case turned out great, she thought, watching
Zebedee tidy his feathers.

If they could just find Honey, things would be perfect . . .

The day of the Pet Show dawned gray and chilly, with
a cold wind and the threat of rain. Andi woke up early.
She'd arranged to take Buddy to Natalie's house to prepare for the show. They'd decided not to go to Clip 'n'
Curl for their free doggy wash because Tristan was still
feeling awkward about visiting the salon. Besides, it was
hard to worry about how Buddy was going to do in the
show when Honey was still missing.

The doorbell rang just after eight o'clock and Andi
ran to answer it with Buddy at her heels. Tristan was
on the step. Behind him, out on the sidewalk, stood
Ella.

Andi's heart sank. She didn't dislike Ella, but she
couldn't imagine Natalie being overjoyed to see her. "Hi,
Andi," Tristan said. "Is Buddy ready for his big day?"

"Yeah. I'll just get his things." Andi had already put

his shampoo, brush, and comb in a carrier bag. Now she just had to pick up the hoop.

Mrs. Talbot came into the hall to see them off. "Good luck!"

"Thanks." Andi kissed her mom, then grabbed her jacket, clipped on Buddy's leash, and scooted out of the door.

Ella and Tristan walked behind Andi all the way to Natalie's house. At first, Andi tried to get involved in the conversation, but whenever she turned around to join in, Ella stopped so there was always a distance between them. Andi was puzzled, but she figured Ella wanted to talk to Tristan alone.

Natalie was waiting for them on the porch, with Jet on his leash. "We forgot to buy ribbon for the dogs to wear round their necks," she said. "Let's scoot down to Main Street now. We should have plenty of time."

This time, Ella stayed a few steps ahead of them as they walked with the dogs bouncing around them.

"I hate to think of the Pet Show going ahead without Honey," Natalie said. "And I hate to think of Windwhistle winning—it wouldn't be fair with Honey out of the running." She sighed. "I'm beginning to think this is one case we're not going to solve. We still can't be sure if Honey's lost or stolen."

"We know Amanda Singer didn't take her," Tristan pointed out.

"And that the other customers aren't likely to be dog-nappers," Natalie added. "But if Honey ran out of the salon, we would have found her. We've searched everywhere! She *must* have been stolen."

"I'm not so sure," Andi said. "Think about it. The commotion happened by accident, right?"

"No kidding," Tristan said. "So?"

"So it wasn't like somebody planned a distraction to steal Honey. And anyway, everyone was busy chasing their own dogs."

"That's true," Tristan said. "But if Honey hasn't been stolen, then why haven't we found her?"

"I have an idea," Ella chimed in.

Andi held her breath, hoping Natalie wouldn't say anything.

"Since you say the dog was tiny, maybe she hid somewhere in the store!" Ella continued.

"We've already searched the salon," Natalie said.

They turned onto Main Street, which was packed with people. Andi noticed a man coming toward her with an empty pet carrier. She tried to move out of his way but the basket caught her painfully in the shins. "Ow!" She rubbed her legs.

"What a huge basket!" Tristan said. "He must have a massive dog."

Andi stared at him. She remembered the time Buddy had scared Amanda Singer's tiny dog. Windwhistle had run into his pet carrier for safety. Maybe Honey did the same thing when she got scared. "Ella's right!" she exclaimed. "Honey might have hidden in one of the pet carriers in the kennels. I didn't think to look inside them."

"But she'd have come out later, when things calmed down," Natalie pointed out.

"Maybe she couldn't get out," Andi said. "Maybe the door got wedged shut or something. We have to check it out. Come on!"

Suddenly they heard a squeal. Whirling around, they saw a golden retriever jumping up at Ella. "Get it away from me," she begged, flailing her hands. "Please!"

The boy holding the dog's leash pulled it away. "Sorry. He's just being friendly," he said.

Ella put her hands over her face and burst into tears.

"What's wrong?" Andi cried, running over. "Did the dog bite you?"

"Don't come near me. Not with Buddy." Ella lowered her hands and backed against a store window, looking terrified.

"Buddy's not going to do anything to you." Natalie joined them, frowning. "Ella, are you scared of dogs?"

"I . . . I'm not scared, exactly. I just don't have any experience with animals. But I'm not afraid, just allergic. And I'm okay with fish."

"How does she know she's allergic if she's never had experience with animals?" Natalie whispered to Andi.

Andi privately agreed, but she didn't say so. Ella was upset enough already.

"What about that stuff you said about helping out at the ASPCA?" Tristan put in.

Ella hung her head. "I made it up. I wanted to have something in common with you guys so you'd like me on my first day. Everything I know about animals, I found out on the Internet."

"We *do* like you," Andi said, ignoring Natalie's glare. "You don't have to make stuff up."

"Come to Clip 'n' Curl with us anyway, Ella," Tristan urged. "You can wait outside if you don't want to be inside with all the pets. If Andi's right, Honey could have been in that carrier all week."

The Pet Finders charged over to the salon, with Ella keeping a good distance from Buddy and Jet. When they arrived, David Nazrallah was standing just inside the door, his eyes blazing. In front of him, Aggie looked pale and worried.

"You will hear from my lawyer about this!" David raged. He turned to leave.

"Wait, David. We think Honey might be here after all!" Andi cried.

She, Tristan, and Natalie squeezed past him and raced along the corridor that led to the kennels. To their horror, the pet carriers were gone.

Aggie, David, and Ella came hurrying in. "What do you mean?" David asked. "How can Honey be here?"

"Where are all the pet carriers from the other day?" Tristan demanded.

"The ones that were in the back? There was a mix-up with the order," Aggie replied. "The supplier sent too many. He came and picked up the extras on Wednesday morning."

"Oh, no!" Andi moaned. "We think Honey might have been inside one of them!"

Chapter Thirteen

The Pet Finders piled into the back of David's station wagon and Ella jumped in the front. There wasn't a moment to lose!

Andi hugged Buddy tightly as they sped across town to the warehouse where the pet supplies were stored. It seemed to take ages to get through the busy Saturday traffic. Even the freeway seemed to be moving no faster than a slow crawl. *Please, please, please let Honey be all right*, she wished silently.

At last, they reached Fernville, a suburb that bordered Orchard Park, and David wove through sidestreets until they reached the warehouse.

"We'll probably have to split up to search," Ella said. "Warehouses can be enormous. I went to one with my dad once to get some stuff for the theater he used to manage, and we were there for hours trying to find everything we needed."

Andi wished Ella would be quiet. Telling them how hard it was to find anything in a warehouse wasn't helpful right now.

David drove into the receiving dock area and jerked to a halt next to a sign that said PET SUPPLIES. They all piled out.

Andi's heart sank. The warehouse was huge—at least the size of an aircraft hangar, and the height of a two-story building. How on Earth were they going to find one tiny dog inside one pet carrier in there?

"Wait here, Bud." Andi lifted him back into the car. "Jet will keep you company. We won't be long." Buddy whined as she shut the door, but Andi knew she couldn't keep an eye on Buddy and search for Honey at the same time.

They sprinted across the yard and hammered on the warehouse door. A sign fastened to the wall showed that it was only open on weekdays between 10:00 A.M. and 5:00 P.M. "I hope there's someone here," Andi said anxiously.

"Open up!" Tristan yelled, banging harder than ever. "It's urgent!"

They heard bolts shooting back and the door opened to reveal an enormous warehouse full of metal shelving crammed with pet goods. The janitor, a skinny man in oversized denim overalls, peered out at them. "What's the trouble?"

"We think there may be a dog in here," Andi said breathlessly.

The janitor frowned. "No, this is a supplies warehouse. We don't store livestock."

"She got trapped in a pet carrier by mistake," Natalie explained. "It was part of a batch that was picked up last week from a salon in Orchard Park. Do you know where they might be now?"

Good work, Nat, thought Andi. That should save searching the entire warehouse!

Still frowning, the janitor shuffled back from the door and pointed into the shadows. "You could try aisle thirty-seven," he said. "Left hand side, about half-way down. We had some returns come in the other day, and that was the only space left."

Andi, Tristan, Natalie, Ella, and David sprinted past the janitor and raced along the aisles. Thirty-four, thirty-five, thirty-six . . .

"This is it!" Tristan shouted, swerving sideways and vanishing between the high stacks of shelves.

Halfway down they found what they were looking for—right where the janitor had said—shelf upon shelf of pet carriers stretching all the way up to the ceiling. "Honey! Can you hear me?" Andi called, throwing open the nearest carrier.

Honey wasn't inside.

Pushing it aside, Andi pulled another carrier off the shelf. It was empty, too.

They all worked frantically, pulling down box after box, knowing that they were racing against the clock. If Honey had been trapped without food or water for four days, she would be in serious trouble.

Every carrier she opened was empty. Andi grew more desperate by the second. "Honey, where are you, girl?" She paused for a moment to listen, but there was no answering whimper.

The bottom two shelves were soon empty and the third shelf was out of reach. "We'll need a ladder," David said.

"I'll go get one." The janitor hurried away. To Andi's relief, he seemed to understand the urgency of their search at last.

"There's no time." Andi scrambled up on a shelf at waist height, then stretched up to grab a shelf support above her head.

"Careful, Andi," Natalie warned. "The shelves are wet in places. I guess the roof must leak."

Andi hauled herself onto the third shelf. There wasn't much space in front of the pet carriers and she held tight with one hand while passing baskets down with the other. Bit by bit, she cleared enough space to work in. Then she checked some carriers herself, shifting them to one side when she'd looked inside. When she reached the back of the shelf, she noticed a glitter of pink below her. "What's that?" she said, peering down.

The bottom shelf was about nine inches off the floor and a bright pink carrier had fallen down behind it. It was lying on its side, half in and half out of a puddle from the leaky roof. Andi slid down behind the shelves and picked it up. Her heart started thudding. This carrier definitely felt heavier than the others. Holding her breath, Andi opened the door.

Inside, lying very still with her eyes closed, was Honey.

"I've found her!" Andi called. With trembling fingers, she reached in, hoping for Honey's sake that she wasn't too late. The tiny dog felt warm, and when Andi rubbed her fur, one eye flicked open and looked up at Andi.

"She's alive!" Andi cried. Cradling the tiny creature

carefully against her chest, she crawled out through the lowest shelf. Honey was so thin, she felt like a baby bird in Andi's hand.

The janitor came back with a stepladder. He stopped when he saw Honey. "Is she . . . ?"

"Alive," David breathed.

At the sound of his voice, Honey opened her mouth and gave a little whimper.

David came over to take her gently in his hands. "Her fur is wet."

"Probably from the roof," the janitor said. "I've been meaning to fix it for ages."

"Actually, you've just saved Honey's life," Andi said. "The rainwater that soaked through her pet carrier kept her alive. Animals can survive that long without food, but not water."

Natalie phoned ahead to tell Fisher that they were on their way. Then they all piled into the car and headed to the ASPCA.

"I saw a movie once about a man who got trapped in a cave for two weeks. He survived by drinking rainwater, just like Honey," Ella said chattily.

Fisher was waiting outside the ASPCA when David pulled up. "Come on in!" he called. "We need to fix up a drip to rehydrate Honey and give her some nutrients to make up for all the meals she's missed. There's no way she'll be fit enough for the Pet Show, I'm afraid."

David shook his head. "That's the last thing on my mind right now."

Andi glanced at her watch. "We'd better go. We haven't even started getting Buddy and Jet ready for the show yet."

Andi, Natalie, Tristan, and Ella sped back to Natalie's house and found Aggie waiting for them. "Mobile dog groomer at your service!"

"We found Honey and she's going to be okay," Natalie told her.

"I know. David called and asked me to help you out. So, let's get these two into the bath!" They ran upstairs with Ella trailing behind.

"Are you all right, Ella?" Tristan asked.

"Yeah. Buddy and Jet seem like nice dogs, but I'll watch what's going on from back here, if that's okay."

The dogs were ready in record time. Jet's gleaming black fur showed off the red ribbon Aggie had tied around his neck. Buddy wore an emerald green ribbon that looked perfect against his sleek tan-and-white fur.

"Wow, Bud," Andi said, hugging him. "You look amazing!"

"Good luck with the show," Ella called as they hurried downstairs.

"Aren't you coming?" Tristan asked.

Ella shook her head. "I might get to feel more confident around dogs with Buddy and Jet to help me, but there'll be too many at the show. I'm not ready for that just yet."

"Thanks for helping us find Honey," Andi said as Ella opened the front door.

"No problem. See you guys on Monday. Bye, Tristan." She gave him a huge smile and then shut the door behind her.

"Phew!" said Natalie. "The nonstop talking drives me nuts."

"She's only trying to be friendly," Andi pointed out.

"I know. And I guess I can put up with her some of the time, but I don't want to hang out with her twenty-four/ seven. In any case, I'm not sure I want to spend time with someone who's got such bad taste."

"You said you liked her clothes!" Andi reminded her.

Natalie grinned and nodded toward Tristan. "I was referring to her taste in boys!"

The Pet Show was in full swing when they arrived back at the ASPCA center. The hall, the parking lot, and part of the soccer field next door had all been converted into rings and collecting areas. "It doesn't seem to matter that some people pulled out," Tristan said. "There are still about a zillion here."

"And the sun's come out, too," Natalie said. "That's lucky, because some of the show rings are in the parking lot."

They squeezed through the crowd, admiring the beautifully groomed dogs in their roomy show cages. They recognized some of them from Clip 'n' Curl and from their Musical Freestyling class. The main show ring had been set up at the end of the hall farthest from the door, with plenty of room around it for spectators.

"Junior Handler Class," announced a voice over the loudspeaker.

Andi gulped. Suddenly her stomach was full of butterflies, and her hands felt clammy on Buddy's leash. Was she about to make total fools of herself and Bud? She took a deep breath and squared her shoulders. Buddy looked fabulous, and she'd practiced his trick until he was probably dreaming about jumping through hoops. She couldn't let him down now. She crouched and patted Buddy's head. "That's us, boy."

Leaving Buddy's hoop with Tristan, she went into the ring. The other competitors looked superconfident, which made Andi even more nervous. So much for the ASPCA wanting to encourage brand-new competitors to take part in dog shows—these guys looked like they'd been competing all their lives! A tall, slender girl with flowing blond hair led an elegant Afghan that seemed a perfect match for her hairstyle, while behind her walked a very serious-looking boy with a bouncing black-and-white collie.

Andi decided she wasn't helping herself by studying the competition too closely.

Following the boy in front of her and his beautiful dalmatian, she walked around the ring with Buddy trotting obediently at her heels. Glancing sideways, she saw her mom, Tristan, and Natalie standing at the edge of the ring. Her mom smiled encouragingly, while Natalie and Tris gave her a thumbs-up.

Buddy sat on Andi's foot and she ruffled his ears, trying not to look at the crowd or at the judge as she worked her way along the row.

She racked her brains to remember everything David Nazrallah had told her about showing dogs: Give the judge plenty of time to look at your dog and listen very carefully to instructions. All judges like smart owners as well as smart dogs!

When the judge reached Buddy, she gave him a quick

look over. "Very nice," she told Andi. Then she returned to the center of the ring. "Please walk your dogs around the ring," she told the contestants.

"Come on, Bud!" Andi said.

"Left turn," called the judge.

Andi turned and was pleased when Buddy followed neatly.

"Fast pace," the judge said.

Andi sped up and Buddy ran with her. "Good boy," she whispered. They'd gotten off to a great start! As they jogged around the end of the ring, she spotted David Nazrallah watching from the back of the crowd. He caught her eye and nodded, as if he thought she was doing well, too.

The judge studied the competitors while they ran, jogged, and walked around the ring, stopping or changing direction on her orders. Andi hardly noticed the other people in the ring: her attention was totally focused on Buddy. At last, the judge told them all to halt. "For a little bit of fun," she explained to the spectators, "we have asked the competitors to work on a simple trick with their dogs." She pointed to the boy with the dalmatian. "Number fifty-one—dalmatian—will you start, please?"

The boy led his dog to the small stage to one side

of the ring. He unclipped his dog's leash then put his hands down on the floor, forming a bridge with his body. He whistled and the dalmatian wriggled underneath him, ran around him and, finally, jumped right over him. The crowd clapped enthusiastically as the boy stood up.

That was pretty good, Andi thought. *I hope Buddy remembers how to jump through the hoop!*

"Number one five five, Jack Russell terrier—you next, please," the judge said, smiling at Andi.

Andi ran across to Tristan with Buddy scampering beside her. She took the hoop from him. "Good luck," he called as she ran to the stage.

The butterflies in Andi's stomach began to flutter furiously as she removed Buddy's leash. There was no turning back now! She held the hoop about six inches off the ground. "Through you go, Bud."

Buddy wagged his tail and sat.

"No! No sitting," Andy whispered. "Come on, boy." She gestured for him to go through the hoop. He stood up, ran toward it, then dodged around it.

A ripple of laughter ran through the crowd.

Andi's cheeks grew hot. "Come on, Buddy," she begged. "Please don't embarrass me in front of all these people. I know you can do this!"

Buddy ran at the hoop again then squeezed underneath it.

The laughter swelled.

This was turning into a disaster! Suddenly Andi remembered how she'd taught Buddy to go through the hoop the first time. "Like this, boy," she said, trying desperately to stay calm. Trying to forget the watching crowd, she crouched down then jumped awkwardly through the hoop. To her relief, Buddy followed.

The crowd cheered, and as Andi took a bow, she spotted Ms. McNicholas clapping from the edge of the arena. Andi gave Buddy a treat then clipped on his leash and jumped down from the stage.

They returned to their place at the side of the ring and watched the remaining dogs perform their tricks. They all behaved perfectly. *We're going to be last by a mile*, Andi thought. "But never mind, Bud," she said as she led him out of the ring. "We did our best!" He'd done really well with the basic showing routine—they'd just run out of luck when it came to doing his trick. *Could dogs get stage fright?* Andi wondered.

When the judge announced the results, Andi and Bud didn't place first, second, or even third. But Andi realized she didn't mind. It was fun just being in the show.

She clapped and whooped with genuine delight as the winners accepted their ribbons.

When all the prizes had been handed out, Andi started to follow the other competitors out of the ring, but the judge asked everyone to wait. "I'd like to award a rather unusual prize for this event," she announced. "The ribbon for the best *human* trick goes to Andi Talbot!"

Andi burst out laughing. "I bet I'm the first *person* who's ever won a prize at a dog show." She and Buddy headed for the stage, while the crowd clapped and clapped. Out of the corner of her eye, she could see her mom, Tristan, and Natalie doing a miniature "wave" with their arms.

"Well done," the judge said, shaking hands with Andi and handing her a green-and-yellow striped ribbon. "I've never seen a person jump through a hoop instead of her dog!"

Andi thanked her, waved the ribbon at the crowd, then ran over to Natalie and Tristan.

"They judged the Best Condition class while you were in the ring," Natalie said, "and Jet came in third." She showed Andi the yellow ribbon fastened to his collar.

"That's awesome, Nat!" Andi exclaimed. "I'm not surprised Jet did so well. His coat is so shiny I can almost see my face in it."

Tristan glanced at his watch. "They'll be judging Best In Show outside," he said. "Come on, we can't miss that!"

As they ran outside, the loudspeaker boomed out: *"The results of the Best In Show competition are ready!"*

"Quick!" Natalie exclaimed.

The Pet Finders darted across the parking lot to the big outdoor ring. Through the crowd, they could see the six competitors who had already won their purebred classes standing in a line. Amanda Singer and Windwhistle were among them.

"And the winner is . . . " declared the announcer, "Windwhistle!"

Everyone cheered and clapped, although privately Andi thought the ribbon would have gone to Honey if she had been able to take part. There was something about the little dog's personality that made her really special—and had probably given her the determination to survive while she was trapped in the carrier.

"There's David," Andi said, spotting him in the crowd.

The Pet Finders wriggled their way through to him.

"Hey, Andi, you did great!" he greeted her, his brown eyes sparkling. "Too bad Buddy decided he didn't want to jump through the hoop, but apart from that, you looked like real professionals!"

"Thanks," said Andi. "Your advice worked, although I'm not sure Bud's got a great show-ring career ahead of him."

"How's Honey doing?" Tristan asked.

"Fisher thinks she might be able to go home later today," he said, sounding pleased. "And it's all thanks to you." His face grew somber. "I really appreciate everything you guys did to find her. I don't know what I'd have done if anything had happened to her."

"Hey, it's what the Pet Finders are for," Tristan said cheerfully. "We're glad we could help—although next time maybe she could pick a smaller warehouse to get lost in!"

David smiled. "I hope there *isn't* a next time," he said. "But if there is, I'll know who to call." He nodded toward the arena. "Windwhistle did well. I should go and congratulate Amanda." He waved at them before turning toward the entrance to the ring.

"I'll bet Honey wins next year," Andi said.

"Me, too," Natalie agreed.

Tristan raised his can of soda. "Well done, Pet Finders, for solving not one but two more cases!"

Natalie agreed. "Not to mention earning free makeovers for Buddy and Jet!" she reminded them.

Andi high-fived each of her friends in turn. "Here's to Honey, Zebedee, and most of all, to us!"